LOVE
MEETS DARK

FIVE
ROMANCE
SHORT
STORIES

SHIRLEY SIATON

LOVE MEETS DARK

Five Romance Short Stories

Copyright © 2025 Shirley Siaton Parabia

ISBN 978-1-961052-19-2 (**paperback,** *romance*)
ISBN 978-621-490-135-7 (**paperback,** *discreet*)

1st Edition, October 2025

Published by Shirley S. Parabia
Romance cover design by RJ Creatives
Discreet cover design by Marika Veil
Interior formatting by Champagne Book Design

Inky Sword Book Publishing
Barangay Quezon, Arevalo, Iloilo City 5000
Republic of the Philippines
inkysword.com

A NOTE FOR THE READER

Thank you for picking up *Love Meets Dark*. As the title suggests, this collection explores the intersection of love and darkness. These stories delve into heavy themes, intense emotional dynamics, and feature characters who sometimes make difficult choices.

While I believe deeply in the hope and healing found within these pages, I want you to be able to make the best and safest reading choice for you. Your well-being is the most important thing.

Please be aware that this collection contains the following themes and potential triggers:

- Explicit sexual content (spice)
- Grief, bereavement, and the death of a spouse/partner
- Stalking (both by a romantic interest and a threatening party)
- Recounted domestic abuse/violence and childhood trauma
- Vigilante justice and revenge killing
- PTSD and nightmares
- Mentions of suicide, cancer, and accidental death
- Poverty and financial hardship
- Power imbalance dynamics

To Peter

Forever my hero,
in shadows and in the light

CONTENTS

LOVE
MEETS DARK

RAIN CHECK

CHAPTER 1

Strong Winds

I T ALWAYS STARTS THE SAME.

The storm barrels in sudden and merciless, rattling the glass windows of the stores of the old commercial building. The wind howls, a large gust sending my umbrella to the side, bent and useless against the raging downpour.

Rain slaps against my skin as I make my way to the corner convenience store. I try to wrestle my umbrella back into place, but I'm already soaked through, shivering as thunder cracks overhead.

I realize the umbrella is broken. I've taped it back together in a few places before, but now the plastic has snapped clean through. Sighing, I toss it into an overflowing garbage can. I tell myself to buy a stronger one next time, but it also means skipping meals for a few days.

By the time I push through the glass doors of the store, I look half-drowned.

And he's there. As always.

I know him as Danny.

I heard a little old lady call him by the name once, while she was buying Vicks and some lozenges.

He's maybe thirty-something, lean and tall, bronze skin glistening where his sleeves are rolled up. He has tousled dark hair he never bothers taming, and eyes so dark they sometimes flash gray in the store's light. Tattoos run along his arms, half hidden by his shirt, dangerous and beautiful all at once.

He looks up from behind the counter, and something in me tightens out of instinct.

My heart pounds, nipples straining under my wet blouse, my body betraying just how much I ache for his attention. I tell myself I only duck into this shop for shelter as I await the mercy of the rideshare or taxi service to take me home.

But the truth is, I always find my way here because of him.

He grabs a towel from under the counter and holds it out without a word. Swallowing hard, I reach for it a little too quickly. When my fingers brush his, heat sparks through me, sharper than the storm.

"Thanks," I manage, hoping he couldn't hear my voice shaking.

This is the fourth time he has done this in the past two months, since I started seeking shelter at his store whenever it rains after my night classes at the College of Law.

"No problem." In contrast to mine, his voice is steady and low-pitched. He slides a paper cup across the counter. "Coffee. On the house. With sugar, right?"

I nod and smile despite myself, wrapping both hands around the cup. The warmth seeps into my chilled fingers. "You don't even know my name, and now you're giving me free coffee?"

"Then maybe you should tell me," he says, leaning just slightly closer.

"Alya," I answer, more breathless than I mean to be.

"Alya." His lips quirk as he repeats the word. "I'm Danny. Pay me back when the sun comes out. Rain check."

I always come to the store at night, but I don't argue.

"Rain check," I echo instead. "Fine."

The heat of the coffee spreads through me, but it's nothing compared to the heat pooling low in my belly from the way he's looking at me. His gaze doesn't wander crudely, but it lingers heavily.

I bring the coffee to my lips, because I need the excuse not to drown in his black-gray eyes. My eyes almost flutter close at how good it tastes.

"Guess I owe you a lot already," I say.

"You don't," he murmurs. "The storms have been brutal lately. A place like this is meant for shelter, anyway. Besides, everyone in the city knows where Montalban Mini Mart is. Easier for your ride to find you."

I meet his eyes. He's looking straight at me, not even blinking. I square my shoulders, trying in vain to push down the blush creeping up my neck. "Still. You didn't have to."

He grabs a black plastic packet from under the counter. He slides it toward me. When I touch it, I realize it's a pair of rubber slippers.

"You're going to wreck those shoes if you go home like that," he says softly.

This time, the blush sets my entire face on fire. "You don't have to do that."

"Only for regulars," he replies smoothly. "You've been in here enough times to qualify."

I bend my head down to hide my face, pretending to set my coffee and bag down on the counter. I slide my feet out of the soaked flats and ease them into the slippers.

"Feels like cheating," I say. "You're giving me too much."

When I look up, he hands me a small bottle of water, shrugging as he says, "Hydrate."

I stare at him, more surprised now than flustered. I want to ask him why he's doing all this. Why he notices my needs when no one else ever does.

Instead, I say, "You're...strangely prepared for rescuing half-drowned strangers."

He chuckles. "Not strangers anymore, Alya."

The sound almost undoes me, so I try to gather myself and do the only thing I could. The one thing he deserves.

I smile.

"No, Danny," I say. "Not strangers anymore."

He smiles right back, and my breath stops for a second.

"Good," he says. "Makes it easier when you show up again next time."

I incline my head, amused at his statement. "What makes you think I will?"

"Because the rain always comes back," he says simply. His gaze holds mine a beat too long. "And so do you."

I feel the flush in my face coming back full force. Just then, my phone pings, letting me know that the driver has reached the store.

I mutter *goodnight* and *thank you*, grabbing my bag, water bottle, and coffee as I go. I don't wait for him to answer.

Because he's right.

I'll be back. He knows it. I know too.

That's how it starts. Towels and coffee. Then he's added slippers and water.

His quiet care. My reckless need to be near him when the world around me is dark and drenched.

And now, the storm is raging louder inside me than outside.

CHAPTER 2

Storm Signal

JUST LIKE ALWAYS, SHE APPEARS.

The moment the rain hits like a hammer against the glass, I know Alya will be at my door sooner than later.

She's gentle-looking and soft-spoken, but I can always see the steel flickering behind her eyes like lightning. She always looks put together even during the heaviest storms, dressed in bright-colored blouses and skirts.

Tonight, as she walks through the glass doors, her long dark hair hangs loose, dripping down her shoulders. Her light brown skin gleams wet under the fluorescent glow. Her umbrella hangs limp and loose from her right hand.

She shivers as she hobbles in, and I'm already reaching for the towel.

"Here," I say without preamble.

"Hi," she says as she takes it. "Me again. Thanks."

Her fingers brush mine, and it's enough to send a shudder straight through me, even though I'm comparatively warm and dry. I grab a paper cup and dispense the coffee from the machine the way she always takes it. As I wait for the cup to fill, I gesture toward the plastic stool I had set up by the counter.

"Sit. Dry off. You waiting for a ride?"

She nods, smiling faintly as she sets down her bag and umbrella on the floor, where I had also set up some hand-woven rugs to keep the surface dry and slippage-free.

"Yeah," she answers. "App says twenty to thirty minutes. I'll try not to flood your floor in the meantime. I like these mats you brought in, by the way. Very colorful."

I nod. "I got them from the market last Sunday. Scraps from tailoring shops, I believe. You seem to like colors, so I took a chance on the brightest-looking ones."

She blushes as she wraps the towel around her shoulders, then averts her eyes to take her coffee from the counter.

"Well, they're very pretty," she says. "I really like them."

"Glad you do," I answer.

She settles on the stool, still not looking at me.

Her voice is soft but curious when she finally speaks.

"This store…it's been here a long time, hasn't it? Feels older than the others on this block. I remember it being around when I first came to the city."

"Yeah," I admit. "One of the oldest in town. My grandparents opened it, then my dad and mom took over eventually. It was supposed to go to my brother, Eddie. He…passed away a while back. So here I am."

Her expression shifts as she looks at me, sympathy threading through her features, but it isn't pity. "I'm sorry. That must have been hard."

I nod. "It was. Still is. But the store's all I've got of my family, so I keep it running. Some of the employees have been with us for decades too."

She tilts her head, studying me. "So you're on your own then."

"I am." The words sit heavy on my tongue. "You?"

She takes a deep breath, as if weighing whether or not to say it. "Me too." Her eyes drop to her hands clutching the cup. "My father…he died years ago."

I don't speak, just wait. She glances at me, then looks away, words spilling like the rain outside.

"We had a farm in the province. He borrowed money from a rich businessman so I could go to college. Put the land up as collateral. He didn't really understand the documents. The businessman who wanted the land… they made sure of that. Well, there were typhoons that pretty much took all our harvests and my father missed more than a few payments. That was that. When they took everything—he couldn't live with it."

Her voice breaks. "My mother found him in the fields. He shot himself through the mouth with his *paltik*."

The breath I let out is ragged. "Alya…"

She shakes her head quickly. "My mother…she lasted a few months. Then a stroke. But I think she was already gone by then." She gives a shaky, humorless laugh. "I was lucky I had an aunt here in the city. She worked at a private school, got me a job in Admin when I finished college. She died two years ago."

Silence stretches between us, broken only by the hum of the refrigerators and the rain battering the glass.

Finally, I ask quietly, "And now?"

"Now it's just me." She lifts her chin, her voice steadier now. "I work days at the school. Go to law classes at night. I go to the college two blocks away. That's why I always find my way here."

"Law school," I echo. "That's no small thing."

Her smile is small, but fierce. "Someday I want to help people like my father. People who don't know the words on those papers. Who sign their lives away because no one explained it to them." Her eyes glisten, but her voice is hard and determined. "I won't let that happen again."

She's so damn brave it hurts. She's so damn *everything* it hurts.

"You're stronger than anyone I know," I tell her honestly.

Her phone pings, cutting through the moment. She glances down, then forces a smile. "My ride's here."

She stands up and hands me her empty cup and the towel back with a grateful nod. After gathering her bag and umbrella, she looks straight at me, eyes still bright with unshed tears.

"You've brought me good luck, you know," she says quietly. "I feel safe in your store. Every time I'm in here, I always manage to get a ride."

I walk her out into the storm, using one of the store's large umbrellas that we keep in our utility closet. The car idles at the curb, headlights slicing through the rain.

Alya pauses, then turns toward me, so close I can feel her heat through the chill.

Her eyes search mine, and before I can speak, she rises on her toes and kisses me.

It's not soft.

It's hungry.

Her lips part against mine, demanding and promising at the same time. A groan rips out of me before I can stop it, my free hand finding her waist, pulling her against me, every inch of her wet body molding to mine.

The kiss is lightning and thunder and everything I've been holding back for weeks since I first laid eyes on her.

She pulls back, breathless, lips swollen. Her smile trembles, but it's real. "Goodnight, Danny. Thanks for everything."

And then she's gone, slipping into the car, leaving

me standing in the downpour with my umbrella, pulse hammering, the taste of her still burning in my mouth.

As I watch her disappear into the rain-drenched night, I already know.

I won't survive another storm without her.

CHAPTER 3

Secret Heat

IT ISN'T RAINING TONIGHT.

The air is still heavy with the day's heat, the sky streaked with thin clouds and the faintest shimmer of stars. It feels weird, walking to Danny's store without a storm pushing me toward it.

My heart beats fast, not from thunder this time, but from nerves. It's payday. I wanted to say thank you. And maybe…I just wanted to see him.

The plastic bag swings in my hand, warm with the weight of fried chicken and mixed meat noodles. I had to wait longer than expected at the restaurant nearby, and panic flutters in me as I hurry down the block.

What if he's already closed up?

What if I miss him?

But the store's lights glow steady. And when I push through the door, he's there.

Like always.

His head lifts, eyes catching mine. That dark, storm-gray gaze pins me.

The first thing he says makes me laugh, breathless with relief.

"It's not raining." His voice rumbles low, a smile forming on his lips as he speaks. "Are you okay?"

I nod, lifting the bag. "I brought dinner. To say thank you."

His smile curves wider, and something inside me falls— falls hard. Right then, I know I'm gone for him. Entirely.

"Dinner, huh?" He chuckles, a sound I want to trap and keep forever. "Guess I should get plates."

He moves to the tiny back office and returns with two mismatched plates and a pair of forks. He takes two cans of iced tea from the fridge and sets them up on the counter, next to where I have laid out the platters of chicken and noodles.

We sit and eat side by side, sharing food and warmth. Outside, the street is silent and still in the late evening. For a moment, it all feels almost ordinary.

"So," I venture, twirling noodles around my fork. "What about before the store? Before you took it over. Did you ever want to do something else?"

His jaw works, but the rest of him stills. "That's a loaded question."

I lean in, heart pounding. "I want to know, Danny. All of it. Whatever you'll tell me."

He sets down his fork, leans back, and breathes out slowly.

His voice is low as he speaks. "I was in prison. Got out a few years ago."

My chest tightens. "Prison? Why?"

His gaze locks on mine, his face expressionless. "Because I killed people. Four of them. For Eddie."

The room lurches, but I force myself to stay still.

"Your brother?" My voice cracks.

"Yeah." His voice roughens, cracking like thin glass under heavy weight. "Eddie was the golden one. Kind, steady, responsible. Took care of me when I was raising hell. Racing bikes, picking fights, wasting time. I was a joke to most people back then. Maybe I still am."

He pauses, dragging a hand down his face. "He was only two years older, but he was always there to pull me back. Keep me going in the right direction. He was my best friend."

I don't say anything when he stops speaking. Somehow, I know he's not done.

"One night, he was walking home after inventory," Danny continues. "Four guys jumped him. Took his money, his phone, his watch. And they stabbed him. Left him bleeding in the street like he was nothing. Knowing Eddie, he would have just given them what they wanted. He would not have put up a fight…unlike me."

A lump forms in my throat, hot and painful. "Oh, God…"

He goes on, his face unchanging. But his voice drops to something that sounds almost fragile.

"My parents were never the same after that. My dad even considered closing this store once, but his friends talked him out of it. And me?" His jaw flexes at the word. "I found them, Alya. Every last one of them. I killed them. One by one. Until there was no one left."

His eyes blaze with a pain that won't burn out, and I watch him, entranced.

"The police caught me after the fourth. I didn't fight it. My lawyer, one of Eddie's closest friends, got me a reduced sentence. I did my years. Got out on parole for good behavior."

He rolls up his sleeve, revealing the ink curling along his arm. "These? From my block. The guards called it Revenge Block. We're the guys who finished the jobs that other people couldn't. Not even our brave boys in blue."

"I was the *mayor* of the provincial jail for a while. It means I survived. You could say I even…thrived."

He looks at me closely, unblinking. "That's why I have the deepest respect for lawyers. If not for one, I could have just rotted away in prison. Because of Attorney Fabregas, I made it back out. Alone, but free for the most part."

I stare, unable to stop the flood of tears. My chest feels split wide open, raw and aching deeply.

"And your parents?" I manage to choke out.

He shakes his head slowly. "Gone before I got out. I came home to nothing but this store." His breath is ragged. "It's all I have left of my family. So I keep it alive. For Eddie. For my parents."

Danny reaches out, his fingers brushing my cheek with a tender hand. "And now…you're here with me." A wistful smile plays at the corners of his lips, the light slowly coming back into his eyes.

The fork slides from my hand, clattering against porcelain. I push back my chair and cross the small space to him. My arms go around his shoulders, holding him tight. He stiffens at first, then exhales.

"I guess you can say I'm lucky, too," he says softly. "Right?"

His arms wrap me up, crushing me against him. His face presses into my neck, hot breath shuddering against my skin.

He smells like soap, rain, and something darker and more dangerous. It only makes me hold him tighter. His heart hammers against mine, and I feel every ounce of his own storm breaking open.

"You're not alone," I say, voice thick with tears. "I'm here."

His grip tightens like he'll never let me go. And then, slowly, he pulls back, just enough to look at me. His eyes burn right into mine, silvery and glittering. My breath catches at the sight.

Before I can speak, his mouth is on mine.

It's rough and desperate, his lips devouring me like he's

been starving for years. A cry escapes me, muffled against his mouth as his hands slide lower, gripping my hips, dragging me onto his lap.

I straddle him without thought, the stool creaking under us as his hands cup my butt, squeezing hard enough to make me gasp. Heat sears through me, pooling low and hot in my stomach, my nipples hardening under my blouse as he presses me closer to him.

"Danny," I whisper against his lips, shuddering as his tongue sweeps into my mouth.

He groans raggedly, and grinds me down against the hard length straining through his jeans.

"You drive me crazy," he rasps. "Every damn time."

I clutch his shoulders, dizzy with need, and kiss him back like I'll never get another chance. Tears and hunger blur together, heartbreak turning into fire, into something I can't fight anymore.

I don't ever want to.

He groans low in his chest, and suddenly his hands are on my waist. He lifts and sets me down on the counter with a roughness that makes me squeal in surprise. The plates rattle, one tips over and clatters to the floor, but neither of us cares.

He reaches beneath my blouse, palms tracing their way over the bare skin of my stomach until his hands cup my breasts under my bra, his thumbs rubbing the nipples in slow circles, making me writhe against him.

"Alya." My name leaves him hoarsely. "Tell me to stop. Tell me and I'll stop."

My hands cup his face, trembling but certain. "Don't stop."

"*Fuck*," he says raggedly. "I'm starving. I'm starving for you."

His hands go lower, down my waist, then moves along my thighs, pushing them open. Then his mouth is on mine again, his hands dragging my skirt higher, higher, until I'm trembling with the exposure, the danger, the need. He kisses down my jaw, my throat, the frantic rise of my chest. Each brush of his lips breaks me open, until I'm shaking, until I can't think.

"Danny," I whisper as he slides off my panties.

"It's okay," he answers. "I've got you. I've always got you."

Then his hand takes over. He caresses and rubs, fingers stroking and moving in and out of me, gently at first, then with more urgency. Under his touch, I feel my body come alive, warm and wet and wanting.

When his head lowers further, his eyes meet mine, dark and burning, asking without words. My answer is in the way I arch toward him, in the way my fingers tangle in his hair.

And then his mouth claims me.

The shock of it rips a cry from my throat, sharp and unrestrained, echoing throughout the store. My body jolts, my knees clamping instinctively around his shoulders, but his grip is firm, holding me wide for him. The first stroke of his tongue is scorching, every nerve in me coming alive.

"Danny—" My voice breaks, begging for more as I lift my hips toward the release that his tongue and lips are promising.

He moans against me, the sound vibrating through every inch of my body, and it undoes me. I tip my head back, clutching fistfuls of his hair, legs jerking helplessly as he devours me. Heat floods in my belly, building fast, too fast, until I'm whimpering his name.

"You taste like heaven," he rasps against me. "You were made for me, Alya. My own heaven."

And then I'm gone, breaking against his mouth, sobbing and gasping for air, every ounce of me ripping into pieces under him. He holds me through it, his hands strong on my thighs, his lips and tongue relentless as he finishes me off, until I collapse back on the counter.

When he finally lifts his head, his lips are slick, his eyes blazing and tender all at once. He kisses my inner thigh, then my knee, then he finally rises.

I'm still shaking when his chin lands above my head, his lips brushing against my hair. His arms cage me on the counter, his breath hot against my cheek, his chest rising and falling.

He's breathing as hard as I am, voice raw when he mutters, "I've been starving, Alya. And I'll never get enough of you."

And I know I'm lost.

I know I am completely, irrevocably his.

That's when it hits me.

He hasn't had anything. He gave me everything, and he's still burning.

His hunger presses against me where our bodies touch.

Now I want to feed him, to take care of him, the same way he just took care of me.

Before I lose my nerve, I slide down from the counter, using his shoulders to pull myself down. My knees sink into the rugs on the floor.

He freezes above me, his eyes going wide. "Alya, you don't have to—"

"I want to," I cut him off, my voice shaky but certain. My hands rest on his thighs, feeling the heat of him through denim. My heart pounds so hard I can barely breathe. "I've never…done this before. But I want to. For you."

He groans, rubbing his hands over his face like he's fighting himself. "Christ. You're gonna kill me."

I swallow hard, fingers fumbling as I push him toward the counter. I feel clumsy and terrified, but determined. His hands hover near my face, as if he's afraid to touch me and afraid to let me go at the same time. When I unzip him and pull down his jeans and briefs, he shudders like the world just cracked open.

Then I see the length of him, rock-hard and red and starving for me. My hands close around him, then I take him into my mouth.

His head tips back, a broken sound ripping from his chest. "Oh, God, Alya…"

Every reaction of his—every gasp, every ragged moan, every jerk of his hips—ignites me. I've never felt power like this, never felt someone come undone because of me. He digs his hands in the counter behind him, muscles locked, body shaking.

I keep going, using my hands, my tongue, my lips, finding a rhythm, my nervousness fading under the rawness of his need. The way he curses under his breath, the way my name falls from his lips—it all makes me braver.

"You have no idea," he gasps out, his hands moving to my hair and his hips starting to thrust in time with my mouth, "what you're doing to me."

The sound of his voice, thick with devastation and desire, makes me feel light-headed. My hands clutch tighter, my whole body humming with heat as I give him everything I can.

And when he finally breaks, when his control shatters and he groans my name like it's the only word he knows, I feel it through every inch of me.

His release is raw, almost violent, but his hands cup my face after, tender and trembling, pulling me up into his arms.

He kisses me almost reverently. "You…you're everything. I don't deserve you, but God help me, I'll never let you go."

I'm breathless and shaking, lips swollen and heart burning, and all I can think is…

I don't want him to.

CHAPTER 4

Sky Falling

THE STORM HASN'T STOPPED SINCE SUNDOWN.

Rain pours relentlessly over the city, rivers crawling down the street, floodwater creeping past the gutters. I ask Willie, the young stockboy who had taken over from his father, to drop off the old cashier, Carmen, and go on straight home. I tell them we might not even open the store in the morning.

They fuss about me staying and tell me to go home, too, but I wave them off. This isn't the first time I've ridden out a storm alone.

But tonight isn't like every other night.

It's past seven. My eyes keep flicking to the clock, then

the door. Alya's classes don't finish until nine, but already my chest is tight, almost restless.

Two nights ago, she brought me dinner and nearly broke me open on the counter with her warmth, her kiss, her touch.

With all of her.

The way she held me after, as if I was worth saving.

I didn't ask for more. I just made sure she got into a car safely before I locked up. But the taste and the feel of her has been burning in me since.

I wait. I pace. The minutes crawl, and the storm only grows worse.

By fifteen past nine, my hands dig into the counter, the same place where I had lifted and stripped and tasted her only nights ago.

But still no Alya.

By half past nine, my pulse is thundering louder than the rain. Rage and fear coil together until I can't sit still another second.

Then the power flickers—and dies.

The store sinks into blackness, thunder splitting the sky.

"Fuck this."

I grab my phone, its glow cutting a pale circle in the dark. I don't hesitate anymore. I lock up fast, splash into the street, the water cold and rising around my boots.

The city is empty. Shuttered shops, no cars, no people. Just storm and silence. I run hard, water slapping up to my calves, until I reach the alley down the block. The garage door groans as I haul it open. My bike waits in the shadows, untouched for months.

"C'mon, baby," I mutter, swinging my leg over. The engine coughs, then roars, vibrating through me. I gun the throttle, spray kicking up as I swerve into the drowned city.

The streets are blacked out, water up to the hubs, but the machine growls steady beneath me.

I ride toward the college, headlights slicing through thick sheets of rain. Every block feels endless. My chest aches with the thought of her out there alone, soaked and cold. By the time I see the faint silhouette of the waiting shed in front of the campus, my heart nearly rips through my ribs.

There she is.

Alya is huddled under the crooked roof, rain tearing at her broken umbrella, water rushing ankle-deep around her. Her hair is plastered to her face, her bag clutched to her chest, but she's still standing.

Still fighting.

The second she sees me, her lips curve in the smallest, fiercest smile.

"I'm glad you came." Her voice is shaky but strong. "The water was too deep to get through to your shop. And no drivers would take me. Said the flood was too high."

I kill the engine, splashing to a stop, water soaking through my clothes.

"It's okay," I rasp, swinging off the bike. "This motorcycle's tough. It can take a little water."

But I don't give her the chance to say more. I reach

her, grab her, drag her against me with a force that's half desperation, half relief. My arms wrap her up tightly.

She gasps against my chest. "Danny, I—"

I cut her off with my mouth. The kiss is wild, rain-slick, teeth and tongue and heat. She tastes like storm and survival, and I drink her down. Her hands clutch at my shirt, holding me just as hard, answering every ounce of my hunger with her own.

When I manage to tear myself away to speak, I don't let her go.

"You're not alone anymore. You hear me? You've got me. Always."

Her eyes shine in the pale light, wet from more than the rain. She nods once, trembling, and pulls me down into another kiss.

This time, it feels like a promise in the middle of the drowned streets.

And I promise myself I'll burn the whole world before I let her stand alone again.

"Don't leave me alone," Alya whispers against my lips, her breath trembling. "Please, Danny. Don't ever leave me alone."

My hands cup her face, thumbs brushing away the rain streaming down her cheeks.

"I won't," I say. "I promise I won't."

"Maybe…this is where I belong," she says, eyes wide as she looks at me. "With you. That's why I keep coming back to the store whenever there's a storm. Because you're the only person I've ever met who makes me feel like I could never be hurt, even when the world is angry."

The confession cracks something inside me. She's shaking, but she keeps talking, almost like a lost girl finding her way home in the dark.

"The first time I saw you," she says, "you got me the coffee I wanted. And you refused my payment. You said 'Rain check, miss.'" Her lip trembles. "You always said it to me, but to me it meant…" Her voice trails off, then she takes a deep breath and continues. "It meant you would always welcome me back, even at my worst. That's why I just kept coming back to you, Danny. I didn't know where else to go."

I pull her against me, arms locking around her small, soaked frame, pressing her head to my chest. My throat is tight, my own eyes stinging. "Alya…"

She buries her face against me, words muffled. "You're the only place I've ever felt safe."

I lower my mouth to her ear. "Then let me take you home. Let me love you the way I've always wanted to."

She jerks back. "What?"

"I love you." My voice is hoarse but steady. "I've loved you from the first storm you walked into."

Her head shakes wildly, rain flying. "How can you say that? I'm nobody. I can't even afford an umbrella half the time. I don't have anything to give you, Danny."

I catch her chin, make her look at me. "No, Alya. I love you because *you* are everything. You're brave, strong, relentless. You walk through storms and still show up. You survived everything, and you're still here." My thumb strokes her cheek, then I trace its path with my lips. "And you're the most amazing and beautiful woman I've ever laid eyes on. You're my everything, even if you think otherwise. I guess I'll just spend the rest of my life trying to convince you."

Something in her breaks open at my words. She lets out a sob, then leaps up, wrapping her arms around my neck, clinging to me like she'll drown if she lets go. I hold her tight, burying my face in her wet hair.

"Take me home," she chokes out. "Get me out of here."

I scoop her up against me, her legs locking around my waist, and carry her to the bike. The engine roars back to life under us, headlights slicing through the flood as we surge into the rising water together.

For the first time in years, I don't feel alone.

CHAPTER 5

Shadow Story

THE RAIN LASHES AGAINST MY FACE AS DANNY DRIVES us through the flooded streets, the motorcycle cutting through dark water.

My arms are wrapped tight around his waist, cheek pressed to his back. Every muscle in him hums with focus, but I can feel the way he eases closer whenever we hit a deeper patch. His body feels like a shield against the storm.

We reach the store's block, an older part of the city where buildings rise narrow and tall. He doesn't stop at the corner but keeps going instead, driving into a wide alley lined with steel gates, their courtyards inside half-drowned. He pulls into one, the engine rumbling low before he cuts it off. My ears ring with silence, except for the endless rain.

"This way," he says.

His hand finds mine and he leads me off the bike, through the arch of the courtyard, toward a worn staircase that creaks under our steps. The power's still out, the building sunk in darkness, but Danny lifts his phone, the small torch casting a pale halo over his face.

Shadows carve along his cheekbones, catching in the wet strands of his hair, and he looks younger somehow. Almost shy.

"This is the way things used to be done here," he says softly, his voice carrying in the stillness. "People lived above or beside their shops. My parents did."

The admission makes my heart tighten. He's always so solid, so strong and infallible, but right now, in the flickering light, I see the boy he once was, still living with ghosts.

The lock of the heavy wooden door clicks open, and he ushers me inside. The apartment smells faintly of wood and rain.

Danny sets his phone on a table and switches on two emergency lamps. The glow from them is warm enough, pushing back the dark.

The apartment is simple and clean, but old. Around me are cabinets with chipped handles, sofas with threadbare arms, and low tables with scratches. The floor is covered with patterned linoleum.

On the wall, framed photographs hang in careful lines.

A couple, most likely his parents, smiling, their arms around each other. A boy who looks similar to Danny but with neater hair and calmer eyes, holding a trophy, his grin easy and kind.

Danny's voice is low as he follows my gaze. "That's Eddie. He always kept this place alive, even when I was being a pain in everyone's ass. My parents…they left it just the way it was. Can't imagine what it must have been like for them. Eddie gone. Then I was put away." He swallows, then looks back at me. "When I got out, I came back here. It still felt like home, even if they weren't around anymore."

He picks up one of the portable lamps, gesturing down the narrow hall with his free hand. "The other rooms are empty. No one's lived in them since. Just me."

I follow him as he leads the way. He stops at a doorway at the end of the corridor.

"This is mine." He runs a hand through his wet hair and tries for a smile as he turns the knob and pushes the door open. "You can stay here as long as you want. No strings attached. Just…home."

The word echoes in me, deeper than I expect.

Home.

Light spills on a small space, with wooden floors and a surprisingly neat bed with white sheets. The walls are bare, lined on one side with worn cabinets. A few books are piled next to a small lamp on the nightstand.

It isn't grand, but it feels safe.

It feels real.

Danny clears his throat, almost awkward now, as he

hands over the emergency lamp. Our fingers brush lightly, but he pulls back.

"I'll try to find something to eat. Might be cold, but it's better than nothing. I've got some clothes in the cabinet if you want to change."

He hesitates at the door, his hand on the frame. In the lamplight, his eyes are softer than I've ever seen them, uncertain. He looks like he's standing at the edge of something he never thought he'd share.

"Get comfortable," he says quietly. "I'll be right outside."

The door shuts behind him, leaving me in the dim glow, my heart pounding.

Then it hits me with the force of the storm outside.

This man, this room, this night…it's all a revelation.

For the first time in years, I feel like I might finally belong somewhere.

The light never comes back on.

The storm presses against the windows, heavy and loud, the rain a constant roar. I move carefully by the glow of the emergency lamp Danny left me.

I peel off my wet clothes, shivering as I pour water from the bathroom bucket over myself. It's cold, but it clears the storm from my skin. I wash off the taste of fear, the weight of the street.

I towel off, then rummage through his cabinet until I

find a pair of old shorts and a plain shirt that hang loose on me but still smell faintly of him.

When I open the door, the hall is aglow with lamplight. Not the chargeable battery lamps from earlier, but real kerosene lamps, their flames flickering gold.

Danny glances up from the table. He's changed, too, into a fresh white shirt and loose dark shorts. His hair is damp, curling at the ends.

"These used to belong to my grandparents," he says, almost shyly, tilting his head toward the lamps on the table. "Everyone had something like this in the old days, I guess."

On the six-seat dining table between us, there are bottles of water and two steaming cups of noodles.

He nods toward a chair. "Not much of a feast, but it's hot. I've got some more boiled water if you want to have coffee later."

We eat in silence at first, rain filling the spaces between our words. Then small talk slips in. We talk about harmless things. The taste of the broth. The memory of storms past and how the building and the store survived then.

He doesn't touch me. Not once.

It surprises me. After everything, after what happened on the counter, I thought…

But maybe he's holding back. Maybe he doesn't want to break whatever this fragile, impossible thing between us is.

When we finish, he gathers the cups and bottles, moving to clean up.

I watch him in the lamplight. Broad shoulders, wet hair,

careful hands, the quiet patience in him…and I can't take it anymore.

I cross the room and press myself against his back, my arms sliding around his waist. He freezes, then slowly turns, setting the dishes aside.

He bends to kiss my forehead, his lips lingering there. "You should rest," he murmurs. "Do you need paracetamol? You've been through a lot tonight."

I shake my head. "No."

He exhales, half a laugh, half in what seems to be disbelief. "I still can't believe you're here. That you're with me and…" His voice falters.

I nod, cutting him off. "Put it away, Danny. All of it. The worry. The doubt. Because yes. I'm here. We're both here. We're home. And I belong with you."

And I see it in his eyes.

The control he's been gripping slips loose. His hands are suddenly on my face, his mouth crashing to mine with a hunger that steals my breath.

The kiss is wild and desperate. I gasp as his hands slide down, gripping my hips, my ass, hauling me up against him. His body is hard and unyielding, his groan tearing through the quiet.

We stumble, then fall together onto the floor, the linoleum cold under my back, his weight pressing me down. His hands are everywhere—palming, clutching, greedy— as he tears my borrowed shirt up over my head and drags my shorts down my legs, stripping me bare in the flickering lamplight.

I arch, helpless beneath him, naked and trembling. His mouth breaks from mine only to trail down my throat, my chest, lower still, until his breath sears hot against the most fragile part of me.

"Danny…" My voice is a soft, pleading cry.

His eyes lift, molten gray in the golden glow.

"Mine," he growls. "You're mine, Alya."

Then he bends and devours me, and the storm outside has nothing on the storm that breaks inside me.

Danny's mouth pulls me apart until I'm shaking, until every breath is a whimper. My body still hums when I reach for him, tugging at his shirt.

"Let me," I whisper, hands clumsy, but more determined than ever.

His eyes darken, breath catching as I peel his shirt away. My palms skim his chest, his skin hot and alive under my fingertips, muscles rippling like coiled ropes of strength. He's beautiful, ink curling down his arms and around his torso, scars etched faintly across his skin.

He's breathtakingly real, a man made of storms and survival.

I touch lower and lower, tentatively, and he groans, catching my wrist but not pushing me away. His restraint shakes through him, but he lets me explore, lets me learn the shape of him with my hands.

"Alya," he rasps. "You don't—"

"Let me," I cut him off. "I want this."

My voice almost falters, but the truth in it steadies me as I pull down his shorts and briefs.

His control breaks. He leans down, kissing me hard, then softer, trailing over my cheek, my throat, my collarbone, his hands cupping my breasts, thumbs brushing over my hard nipples until I arch helplessly beneath him. His mouth follows, hot and hungry, worshipping me in ways that leave me gasping.

He lingers between my thighs, caressing and teasing and licking, until I'm undone again, pleading for him without words.

Then he stills.

Rain hammers the roof, thunder rolls, but his whisper cuts through everything.

"I love you, Alya."

My breath catches. "Danny, I—"

"I love you," he says again, fiercer this time. To my ears, it sounds like the only truth he's ever known. "From the first time I saw you walk into my store and my life. From the first rain check. Always."

Tears sting my eyes, mingling with sweat. I wrap my legs around him, pulling him closer, needing him. Needing this.

"Then take me," I breathe. "Because I love you too."

His mouth claims mine as he gently lowers himself over me. His hands cradle my face and stroke my hair as he slowly enters me. He lets me adjust, waiting patiently with kisses and soft, soothing whispers.

I clutch him tight as I feel him inside me, my body molding to his, then I begin to move. My hips meet his and he groans and curses, then he matches my rhythm with thrusts that become harder, faster, and more desperate.

The world narrows to the heat of his skin, the press of his chest, the worship in his eyes, the pleasure that sears throughout my body as he pounds into me.

His mouth finds my breasts, his name falls from my lips, and I give myself to him completely, wrapped around him as the night swallows us whole.

And in the darkness, in his arms, I finally understand what it means to be home.

CHAPTER 6

Stolen Kiss

THE STORM OUTSIDE DOESN'T LET UP, BUT INSIDE, I can't get enough of her.

Alya is under me, around me, trembling and fierce, and every time she gasps my name it's like a match striking inside my chest. I'm starving, and I know it shows in the way I kiss her, the way I can't stop touching her, the way I keep pulling her back when she tries to breathe.

We burn through the night, moving like the storm wind itself is chasing us. The linoleum floor becomes too small, so I lift her and set her on the table where we ate not an hour ago. The bowls and bottles scatter to the floor, and she laughs breathlessly before I swallow the sound with my mouth.

Her laughter, her tears, her cries—I take them all, because they're mine now, every one.

When the table groans, I carry her again, settling her on the sofa, sinking into the worn cushions with her spread across me, my hands holding her by the ankles as I take her more slowly, more deeply.

And when we're done that way, I ask her to get on top of me.

The flickering lamplight paints her skin gold, and I can't stop staring at her. Alya's hair is loose and wild around her, her eyes still heavy with need, her lips swollen, but she rides me like a goddess as I squeeze her breasts, surprisingly full for someone as petite as her. She leans down to kiss me, and I think I could die like this, drowning in her.

But even the sofa can't contain us. I press her gently against the wall, her body arching into mine, her nails digging into my back, and I whisper against her ear, "You're everything. Do you know that? You're everything."

She whispers it back, and the sound tears me apart. I pound into her harder, mouth lowering to take her nipple, and she cries out, rubbing up and down, taking every inch of pleasure I am giving her.

By the time I carry her into my room, we're both shaking, but I still want more. I set her down on my bed— the bed I've slept in alone for years, the bed my parents kept waiting for me while I was locked away—and tonight, it finally feels alive.

She looks at me, wide-eyed, uncertain but brave, as I bend her on all fours at the edge.

I know I have to show her. Not just what it means to be touched, but what it means to be loved completely.

Then I take her from behind, my hands going around to cup her breasts, my lips and teeth nipping at the back of her neck.

I guide her, teach her how to move with me, how to let go of the fear, how to give in to the hunger that's been between us since the first storm.

Every time she hesitates, I hold her. Every time she falters, I kiss her. And when she grows bolder, when she learns the rhythm of us, I almost lose myself in the wonder of it.

We make love and fall together through the night, over and over, until the storm outside fades into the gray hush of dawn, until she collapses on top of me, her body tangled with mine, hair damp against my chest, breath warm on my skin. I stroke her back, slowly and lightly, as the sun begins to rise behind the curtains.

For the first time in years, I don't feel restless. I don't feel haunted. I feel…whole. Because Alya is in my arms, and she's never leaving.

I kiss the crown of her head, whispering into her hair as sleep finally drags me under.

"I love you. Always."

And she stirs against me, murmuring her answer, "I love you too."

The first thing I notice is the quiet.

No pounding rain, no cracking thunder, no rushing water. Just the soft hum of a city wrung out by a storm.

Then I see her next to me.

Alya's curled into me, hair spread like ink across the pillow, her cheek pressed against my chest.

My arm is numb beneath her but I don't dare move. Not yet. I just watch. The rise and fall of her breath. The way she clutches the blanket like she's afraid it will slip away.

I've always woken up alone. In prison. In this apartment. In silence. But now…now there's someone beside me. Someone warm. Someone real.

Someone I love.

Her lashes flutter, and then her eyes blink open, soft and sleepy, finding mine. For a second, we just stare at each shyly, like two kids caught doing something forbidden.

Then she gives me the smallest smile, and I'm done for.

"Good morning," she whispers.

"Good morning," I manage, my voice rough.

A sharp ping breaks the spell. She leans across me to grab her phone from the nightstand, the blanket slipping, her bare breast brushing my shoulder. I bite back a groan. She scans the screen, then laughs softly.

"School's closed. Flood's too bad in the city to go

anywhere." She sets the phone down, looking back at me, eyes gleaming.

I raise a brow, smirking. "Well. Looks like you're stuck with me."

She giggles, light and unguarded. And before I can blink, she swings a leg over, straddling me. My breath leaves me in a rush.

"Alya…"

Her lips brush mine teasingly, then her tongue flicks out to trace my lower lip. "Rain check?"

Heat slams through me, shattering any control I thought I still had. I grip her hips, my head falling back against the pillow with a helpless laugh. "Hell, no."

She shifts her weight just enough to make me groan, her hair falling like a curtain around us. The blanket slides off her body, and her skin feels like warm silk against mine. My body responds before I can think, hard and aching beneath her.

Her smile tilts wickedly. She rocks once, very slowly, and I choke out a sound I haven't made in forever.

"You're a greedy goddess," I rasp, clutching her thighs, staring up at her like she's a vision I don't deserve.

Her eyes glimmer with mischief and fire. "Why else do you think I keep coming to you? Every single time?" She grinds again, teasing and tormenting. "I know what I want."

A curse breaks from my throat. My hands grip her harder, sliding up her waist, her back, her breasts, desperate not to lose my mind.

"You're killing me," I groan.

"No," she whispers as she leans down, her mouth ghosting over mine. "I'm keeping you alive."

And she's right. Every move from her body, every taunt in her voice, every kiss she steals…it's life itself.

A life we might just live in love, through whatever storms may come.

I surge up, sealing my mouth to hers, tasting her laugh, her moan—all of her. The blanket tangles, the room spins, and I know I'll never get enough.

I'm hers. Always.

No rain checks.

Not ever.

THE MAN
IN THE
SHADOWS

CHAPTER 1

The Crowd

I NOTICE HIM BEFORE I EVER HEAR HIS VOICE.

Megaworld on a Tuesday night is crowded, neon lights splashing the rain-soaked pavement. I'm balancing grocery bags from picking up essentials after work, irritated at myself for forgetting an umbrella, when I see him for the first time.

At first, it's a presence, a strong and undeniable pull.

Then I look toward one of the refreshment stands.

The sight of him hits me like a bolt of lightning.

He's tall—taller than most people rushing around us. He has short, neatly-styled hair, falling over a wide forehead. His shoulders and chest look impossibly broad and strong under his charcoal shirt.

But it's his eyes that hold on to me like invisible chains.

They're deep-set on his face, slightly narrowed, fixed on me like I'm the only thing worth looking at. His lips, shaped like something sensuous and sinful, curl into what could only be a smirk.

I take a deep breath. Then, with a scowl at everything and nothing at once, I rush off.

The second time, I spot him at the bus stop near Festive Walk. He doesn't even pretend to be casual.

He's just there. Waiting.

Watching.

By the third, I snap.

I march up to him outside the mall entrance, my bags cutting into my palms.

"Are you following me?" I demand without preamble.

He doesn't flinch. His mouth curves in response. His voice comes out in a measured, richly textured drawl. "Yes."

My stomach drops. "You're not even embarrassed to admit that?"

"No." His response is even, threaded with something dangerous. "I told myself I'd just watch. That it would be enough. But it isn't."

My pulse is a thunderous mess.

I glare at him. "Why me?"

"Because I saw you once and couldn't stop watching you. You were looking up at all these towers that belonged to other people, and all I could think was they should belong to you instead."

I laugh nervously, trying to think of something equally ridiculous as a clapback. "You own one of these buildings, don't you?"

His lips twitch. "Three, actually."

"Oh my God. What are you, some kind of stalker CEO?"

The words come out sounding more of a Wattpad fever dream than intended.

"Yes," he says simply. "But only yours."

I roll my eyes. "You've got to be joking."

"No, I'm not," he answers, deadpan. He inclines his head toward my bags. "Can I help you with those?"

I shake my head as I continue walking to my stop. Unfazed, he keeps up with me easily, one stride equivalent to two and a half of mine. I don't know whether to laugh or scream at the insanity of the situation.

When the bus arrives, he gestures to the black SUV parked at the curb, in one of the reserved spots that only VIPs could access. "Let me drive you home, miss."

"No, thanks," I mutter, stepping up into the bus. "I'm fine."

For a second, I think I see something flicker in his eyes.

It's definitely not anger, or even disappointment.

He just regards me patiently, then lowers his head in an exaggerated farewell nod that looks more like a knightly bow.

I don't know if I should just give in to the weakness in my knees or throw something at him. But even the canned corned beef in my reusable grocery bag is too eye-wateringly expensive to waste, especially when it will last me at least four square meals. Or six, if I can get a potato from my landlady.

But I can't take my eyes off him as he watches the bus drive off, not moving from his spot on the sidewalk.

CHAPTER 2

The Rain

THE NEXT TIME I SEE HIM, IT'S RAINING HEAVILY. I leave my office and find him waiting under the awning, holding an umbrella big enough for two.

"You again," I mutter.

"Me again," he says easily. He doesn't offer excuses.

I should walk away. Run, maybe, or call our security guard at the bank. But instead I stand rooted to the pavement, fighting the wild heat churning in my stomach.

"You don't even know me," I say.

His gaze doesn't waver. "Then let me."

I meet his eyes without blinking. "I don't really know if I should."

He gestures to a coffee shop down the block. "Let me buy you coffee and something to eat. Least I could do. Catching your bus in this weather would be a nightmare."

I sigh, and nod without saying anything, knowing he's right. Inwardly, I'm berating myself for saying yes to a man who is pretty much stalking me.

We sit side by side at a corner table. The downpour outside lashes against the glass, trapping us in a little bubble of dark and warmth.

"What's your name?" he asks.

"Thea."

"I'm Noah," he offers. The name fits him—solid, old-fashioned, biblical almost.

He stirs his black coffee without drinking it. "Tell me something real, Thea."

I can only blink at him. "What?"

"No small talk. Tell me something I shouldn't know."

I shake my head, laughing nervously as I stir my own cappuccino. "That's a lot to ask from a stranger."

"We're not strangers," he says. "Not anymore."

His intensity should unsettle me. Maybe it does. But it also draws me in, like a strong whirlwind I can't fight.

Against my better judgment, I say, "I don't go home to Negros if I can help it. My family...my father. It's very complicated."

Something flickers in his eyes. "Then don't go home. Stay where you want to stay."

"And where's that?" I challenge.

His answer is quiet, but the words are lethal. "With me."

I feel scorching heat take over my entire body, from the pit of my belly to the tips of my hair.

"Tell me something about you, too," I say, looking away so he can't see how red my face has become.

He doesn't respond at first. Instead, he reaches for my chin with his index finger, turning my head gently to look back at him.

"People stay close to the money," he says softly. "Not to me, Thea. Never for me."

Something twists in my chest. For the first time, he doesn't look mysterious and untouchable.

He looks human.

"I'm sorry," I say honestly.

"Don't be," he replies. "I've learned to read people that way. I see them coming from kilometers away."

I can only nod, watching him as he picks up his cup of coffee and takes a sip.

I finish my cappuccino in silence, too, but it's not the kind that's awkward. It's the kind of quiet that breathes and waits and doesn't ask for anything.

When we leave the coffee shop, the streets are slick with rain. The neon lights of Megaworld paint the puddles pink and gold. He walks me to the bus stop, my lunch tote in his hand, umbrella angled more over my head than his.

"You're insane, you know that?" I mutter, unable to keep from smiling like an idiot.

"Maybe." His eyes glint. "But only for you. You should know that by now."

When the bus arrives, I hesitate, caught between nerves and want, between common sense and something that feels like fate.

He leans down, voice a whisper just for me. "Tell me to stay away, Thea, and I'll disappear. You'll never see me again."

My heart races. I should say it.

But I don't.

The truth, bold and a little crazy, escapes my lips instead. "Don't you dare."

The smile that breaks over his face is enough to take my breath away.

And when he kisses me right there under the rain, softly, almost hesitantly, the city fades until there's nothing left but the two of us.

That night, I dream of him, holding me in the dark, telling me to stay with him.

For him.

CHAPTER 3

The Drizzle

I T DRIZZLES THE FOLLOWING NIGHT.

I step out of the bank and he's there. His umbrella is tilted toward me, raindrops sliding down the sleeve of his shiny gray polo shirt.

"Didn't think you'd be here," I blurt out, heart expanding in a strange kind of relief at seeing him.

"Come on," he answers casually. "It's dinner time."

My stomach betrays me with a loud growl. He gives me a smug, knowing grin in response.

"Fine," I say. "You're buying."

He brings me to a restaurant in the mall with tall glass windows and warm lights, a place too expensive for me to ever go into on my own. It's the kind of place where the waiters seem to glide instead of walk.

The staff and some of the customers, all beautiful women and men, greet him by name.

"Is this your restaurant?" I ask, incredulous.

"One of them," he admits. "This is my youngest baby."

I shake my head, laughing softly. "Of course it is."

A statuesque woman with gray hair piled on top of her head guides us to a corner booth with velvety soft dark blue seats, then backs away gracefully after giving us shiny tablets of the menu. A minute later, a waiter who looks like J-Hope of BTS serves us glasses of iced tea, complete with lemon slices and tiny paper umbrellas.

I try not to gawk at the prices of the food and drinks. "What else do you own, then? Half of Megaworld?"

He smirks. "Only the parts worth keeping."

I snort, then cover my mouth. "Sorry. That sounded rude."

"No," he says, leaning back in his chair. "I like the way you say what you mean."

My cheeks and neck burn at his compliment, so I save face and ask him to choose for me a dish on the menu he thinks I would like best.

Noah orders chicken mushroom soup and a beetroot salad for our shared starters, then sirloin for himself and baby back ribs for me.

Over the smoothest, tastiest soup I have ever tasted, he

studies me in that unblinking way he has, and it makes me spill things I never meant to.

"I grew up in Escalante City," I confess, tracing the rim of my glass. "Every fight, every slammed door, every bruise my mother tried to hide…it all felt louder there. She used to lock me in a dark room whenever my father got home drunk, telling me if I can't see anything it would make it less real. Well, I came here because…I thought if I was far enough away, maybe the sounds wouldn't follow me."

The words taste bitter, but he doesn't look away. He doesn't pity me either. He just listens.

"You've been running," he says quietly.

"Yes," I admit.

"Does it help?"

I huff out a laugh. "Some days. I do my best."

When the main course arrives, he surprises me by offering his plate first. It's a thick, juicy cut of steak. "I got the recipe from a pit master in Arizona. He uses ground coffee beans along with other spices to rub onto the meat. Try it."

I stare at him. "You don't strike me as the sharing type."

"Maybe only when it's you," he says, and it's so blunt my fork tumbles over the ribs on my plate, soaking the handle in sauce.

He chuckles at my expression, then sobers. "I've been alone for a while too. Different reason. My parents separated long before all this. Other people… well, they like to know what I own, not who I am."

"Who are you, then?" I ask before I can stop myself.

His gaze pins me where I sit. "That depends. Who do you need me to be?"

My chest tightens. I look down at my plate, pretending my heart isn't hammering.

"You can't just…say things like that," I mutter.

"I just did." His voice is calm, but there's something beneath it, something dark and unhesitating.

I look back up at him. "I need you to be who you are to me."

"And what's that, Thea?"

"Someone honest. Someone who's not afraid to step out of the dark and tell me things other people try not to say."

He raises an eyebrow, the corner of his mouth quirking in a half-smile. "I've already done that. Surprises me you're still here, actually, in spite of it."

I reach across and tap his nose with my index finger. "You have no idea, Mr. CEO. You don't even know what you've gotten yourself into."

That makes him laugh, a rich, rolling sound that rumbles off his chest and makes me smile right back.

By dessert, a large bowl of *crème brûlée* that J-Hope serves with two golden teaspoons, I'm giggling despite myself. Noah tells me about nearly burning down a kitchen in a hotel in Los Angeles when he was eighteen. I admit I once stole mangoes from my neighbor's tree and blamed it on the cat, then at the typhoon.

For a moment, it feels normal. Just a man and a woman sharing a meal. A very expensive one, but still.

As we get ready to leave, Noah leans in, voice quiet but unshakable. "Don't mistake this for coincidence, Thea. I'm not here by accident."

And I believe him.

The rain has stopped by the time he pulls up the SUV outside my boardinghouse in Mandurriao.

It's the kind of place you only live in if you're desperate: peeling paint, tiny rooms, the echo of other people's arguments through thin walls. I expect him to make a face or make a comment.

He doesn't.

Instead, he kills the engine of his car and steps out to open my door. My shoes squelch against the wet pavement, and suddenly I feel small beside him—me in my white-collar uniform and department store footwear, him in a sleek jacket that probably costs more than six months' rent.

At the gate, he pauses and takes my hand. His grip is warm and steady.

"You need anything?" His thumb brushes my knuckles like it's a habit already.

I shake my head too quickly. "No."

Something changes in his eyes. It's neither disappointment nor acceptance, but something sure, almost determined. But he doesn't say anything.

Instead, he bends and presses his lips to the back of my hand. A kiss so old-fashioned, my knees nearly buckle.

"Goodnight, Thea."

My voice is a shaky whisper when I answer. "Goodnight."

I slip inside the gate, but I look back. He's still there, leaning against his SUV, watching. I raise my hand in a small wave. He lifts his in return, slowly.

Neighbors gather at their gates and peek out of their windows, whispering behind their hands. Eyes flick from me to Noah's car and back again.

I ignore them. My pulse is still caught in my hand where his mouth touched.

I watch him back the car out of the narrow street, then wave again just before he drives off into the night.

I know exactly what I need, but I couldn't tell him.

Because it's him.

CHAPTER 4

The Blackout

IT RAINS HARDER THE NEXT DAY.

My colleagues chat idly during coffee breaks about another typhoon coming in, this time stronger than the one that hit Iloilo less than a month ago.

By the time evening comes, sheets of water blur the streetlights, turning the city into liquid glass.

When I step out of my office after a month-end closing that feels dragged out, I see Noah's SUV parked outside the bank.

This time, he doesn't even ask. He just gets out, umbrella already open, hand outstretched for me.

I take it. This time, he kisses me on the cheek.

He takes me to another restaurant, different from last night's. The other place—his "oldest baby"—is smaller and more intimate, tucked into a quiet corner near the Esplanade. Despite the weather, the other tables are occupied by couples, all speaking in whispers over their drinks.

I watch the soft golden lights flicker against the glass as rain streaks down the windowpanes. Seated from across me, he reaches out and takes my hand.

"Yes?" I ask, trying to cover the nervous flutter in my chest.

"You're so beautiful," he says.

I roll my eyes, but my face is hot.

"I'm not kidding," he insists. "This is how I first saw you, you know. It was around sunset. You were looking at my building. The light hit the glass, and then it fell on you. You looked like you glowed—no, you looked like you're fire itself."

I can only shake my head, unable to speak.

"You weren't even looking at me, Thea," he continues, his eyes locked onto mine. "You were looking at the glass and the light and the shadows, but I wanted you to look at me like that. I was going to give you all the towers you wanted just so I can see you looking like fire."

"I'm sure you're disappointed," I manage to say, keeping my voice light.

"Disappointed?" he echoes, chuckling. "Quite the opposite. I got exactly what I wanted."

I freeze at his words. "What do you mean? What did you want?"

Noah smiles. "I wanted someone to look at me like I'm glass and light and shadows."

"And?" I whisper.

"And you did. You do."

I nod. "Because you're all that and more. Just like me. Maybe that's why…"

"Maybe that's why we found each other?" he finishes. Something raw threads through his words.

I nod again, a lone tear sliding down my cheek.

In a split second, he's crouching next to me, pressing a gray handkerchief to my eyes.

"Don't," he murmurs, his other hand smoothing down my hair. "Don't cry. Please."

I can't look at him, so I take the handkerchief and pat away the tears. "You don't even know me."

"I know enough." His voice is low. "I know you're brave. I know you ran and you survived. I know you laugh when you don't mean to. I know you pretend you don't need help even when you do."

My throat closes. "How could you possibly know all that?"

"Because I've been watching. I've been listening to everything you say and don't say."

It should terrify me. Maybe it does. But more than anything, it makes me feel seen.

Our food arrives just in time. We eat in companionable silence, then he gently guides me to the car.

By the time the SUV rolls up to the boardinghouse, the storm has gutted the street. Every window is black, the rain hammering against the tin rooftops like heavy fists.

"There's no power," he says softly. "The rain must have knocked it out."

Noah is out of the car the moment he shuts off the engine. He takes the umbrella from the back seat and moves to the passenger side. The air feels heavy as I step out onto the flooded pavement. The neighbors have all retreated indoors, the faint glow of lamps and candles flickering dimly behind shutters and curtains.

He guides me through the gate, the beam of his phone torch barely cutting through the dark. We step inside the narrow hallway together.

I feel the shadows close in. The water dripping from my jacket onto the cracked tiles feels like a roaring sea instead of a puddle.

My chest feels tight. Too tight.

At my door, I fumble with the keys. My hand is shaking. The darkness presses too tightly.

"Noah," I whisper. My throat feels raw and dry. "Don't…"

He moves closer. "Don't what?"

My voice cracks when I answer. "Don't leave me in the dark."

For a heartbeat, the space between us roars louder than the rain outside. Then something in him breaks free.

He takes my face in his hand, tilts it up, and kisses me.

It isn't tentative. It's fire.

It's our restraint breaking like glass.

His mouth moves against mine with raw hunger, but his hand stays gentle, thumb stroking my cheek as though I'll shatter.

I gasp, and he swallows the sound, pressing me back against the door. My keys slip from my fingers and clatter to the floor. I don't care.

My fists bunch in his damp shirt, pulling him close, needing him closer. His body is all strength, steady and unyielding, the kind of weight that feels like safety instead of danger.

"Thea," he rasps between kisses, cheek pressed to mine, breath hot on my skin. "Say no, and I'll leave. Just one word."

"Don't go," I whisper desperately. "Please don't go."

Lightning splits the sky outside, throwing his face into sharp relief. For a split second, I can see the wet hair plastered to his forehead, the hunger in his eyes, the fierce tenderness he's trying and failing to hold back.

He groans low in his throat, then his arms are around me, lifting me like I weigh nothing. My legs wrap around his waist instinctively. The movement knocks a breathless laugh out of me before his mouth steals it.

Everywhere he touches ignites. My back. My hips. The curve of my thigh. His hands are careful, but the tension in his grip tells me he's holding back more than I can imagine.

"You're mine," he murmurs against my ear, the words

almost lost to the thunder. "You don't have to be afraid anymore."

I bury my face against his shoulder, trembling from the flood of want rushing through me like the downpour outside. "Then don't let me go. Stay in the dark with me."

His answer is another kiss, deeper and hungrier, one that leaves me breathless and aching and certain.

The wind howls. The boardinghouse creaks. But for the first time in years, the dark feels like shelter.

Because Noah is in it with me.

And when he carries me out of the hallway, I don't care where we end up.

As long as I'm still in his arms.

CHAPTER 5

The Promise

H IS APARTMENT SMELLS OF MINT AND COFFEE.

I barely remember him carrying me to the car and driving off. He doesn't stop driving until we reach a high-rise condominium building, where he parks underground and carries me into the elevator.

As we enter his penthouse unit, warm light spills from a single lamp, falling on steel and glass fixtures. Dark couches and cushions that look impossibly soft form a circle in the middle of the room.

I've barely stepped inside before Noah's arm goes around my waist. His touch feels like he's been holding this back for far too long.

"Are you sure?" he asks me softly.

"I'm sure," I answer, leaning against him. "I want this. With you."

Something in his eyes shatters. The next second, he's kissing me. It's not a careful brush but a deep, hungry drag of his mouth over mine, his palm cupping my jaw. My hands slide up his chest, fingers clutching at his shirt. I can feel his control like a tremor under his skin.

He breaks the kiss just enough to murmur against my lips, "I'll stop if you want me to."

"I don't want you to stop," I breathe, my whole body shaking. "Please, Noah."

The sound he makes is raw and guttural, then he's pressing me against the cool wall. His mouth trails down my throat, his teeth grazing just enough to make me gasp. His hands settle on my hips, lifting me so my toes leave the floor, my skirt riding up. The power of it steals my breath.

"You're mine, Thea," he rasps against my neck. "Tonight and every night after. I'll take very good care of you. I promise."

"Yes," I whisper. "Please."

He curses under his breath. Then his hands are on my thighs, dragging them around his waist. He lifts me and carries me across the hall and into the bedroom, setting me on the edge of the large white mattress. He kneels in front of me, fingers tracing the inside of my knees, his eyes dark and searching.

"I'm going to touch you," he says quietly. "I'm going to make you feel good. And if it's too much, tell me."

I nod, biting my lip, and his mouth finds mine again. He goes slow at first, coaxing and guiding. His hands slide up under my damp blouse, skimming my ribs, pausing just below my breasts. He watches my face, waiting. When I arch into his palms, he groans and covers my skin fully, thumbs circling my nipples through my bra.

Then he kisses me.

This time, it's rough, hungry. He presses me back onto the bed, his body caging mine, his mouth trailing down to my collarbone, biting and sucking lightly, then soothing with his tongue until I'm trembling beneath him. His hands are already at the waistband of my skirt, tugging it down inch by inch, his fingers grazing my thighs with every movement. Then he unbuttons and slides my blouse off, followed quickly by my bra.

"You're so beautiful," he growls, nuzzling each breast in turn. "So fucking beautiful."

I shudder, reaching for him as he licks and sucks my nipples, and the world narrows to the press of his weight, the heat of his breath, the sound of rain against the window.

He kisses down my stomach, then looks up at me from between my thighs.

"You're shaking," he murmurs.

"It just that…I haven't done this before."

He pauses for a moment, then kisses my inner thigh. "Then let me show you what it means to be wanted."

He peels my panties down and slides them off with agonizing care. Then his mouth is on me, scorching hot, his tongue circling slow and low. I cry out, startled, my hips lifting off the bed.

"Easy," he murmurs against me. "Let me."

He eats like a man starved. His hands grip my thighs, holding me wide and open, and I feel everything. Every drag of his tongue, every groan he gives when I tremble, every low curse when I gasp out his name.

When he finally pulls away, I'm dazed and panting hard. My legs fall apart, shameless and wanting. He doesn't take his eyes off me as he unbuttons his shirt, then pushes down his dark slacks and briefs in one smooth motion.

Finally, he stands naked before me.

And my God, he does.

His body is corded with muscle, like carved marble beneath brown velvet, from his impossibly wide shoulders and chest tapering to narrow hips and strong, lean legs.

Between them, I see all of *him*.

He's big. Hard. Thick enough to make my breath catch.

His jaw clenches as he watches my face.

"I'll go slow," he says, voice tight. "I'll never hurt you. You know that, right?"

I nod, then say, "I want you too."

I rise from the bed, bare and trembling, alive in a way I don't have words for. He watches me with fire in his eyes, but he doesn't move. He just breathes, shoulders tense, like he's holding himself back for my sake.

That restraint undoes me more than anything else.

I move toward him on my knees, my pulse slamming against my throat. I reach out and touch him, the muscles of his stomach tight and trembling under my fingers. I rest a hand on his thigh and feel the jolt that goes through him.

"I want to taste you," I whisper.

He blinks hard. "Fuck, Thea…"

"I need to."

Then I lower my mouth. I take a deep breath, and slide him between my lips.

His hand flies to my hair. He lets out a moan that's half agony, half pleasure.

I take my time. I explore him like my own delicious secret. I don't really know what I'm doing, but I want to learn. I want to know how to make him fall apart.

And somehow, I do. I pump him in and out of my mouth. I cradle the soft weight of his balls between my hands as I suck. I feel his hips buckling, his hands pulling at my hair, as he swears and mutters my name.

"Stop," he growls. "Stop. You're gonna make me come right now."

I pull back, licking my lips, stunned.

"You're shaking," I murmur breathlessly.

His eyes are almost black now. "I want it to be inside you, baby."

I nod. My body is trembling for something—and I know exactly what it is.

He pushes me back onto the bed and slides over me,

eyes never leaving mine. One hand braces beside my head. The other guides himself to my entrance, where I'm wet and warm and aching for him.

"Just the tip," he says softly. "You'll tell me if it hurts."

I put my arms around his neck, settling my face against his shoulder. "I trust you."

The first press is a small burn, a stretch that makes me gasp until I almost sink my teeth into his skin. He stills instantly, a curse spilling from his mouth.

"You're so tight," he groans. "Jesus, Thea, your body's holding me like it never wants to let go."

I dig my fingers into his back. "Don't stop. Please. I want all of it."

His control fractures. He thrusts deeper, slowly, inch by inch until he's buried to the hilt. We both moan at the feeling. My body clenches around him, the fullness overwhelming, the pleasure riding on the edge of too much.

He holds still for a moment, lips in my hair, his breath coming fast.

"Fuck, you feel so perfect," he says. "You're mine now. You know that, don't you?"

I nod, tears pricking at my eyes. "Yours."

And then he moves.

Slowly at first, dragging almost all the way out before sinking back in with a shudder. But it doesn't take long before his rhythm changes, before he starts to take me in earnest, each thrust stealing my breath.

"You take it so well," he rasps. "You're so perfect, baby. So goddamn tight."

He grips my wrists and pins them above my head with one hand, his other arm anchoring me as his hips slam into mine. The bed creaks beneath us, the headboard hitting the wall with every thrust. I cry out as pleasure begins to roll around me in waves.

My back arches, and I whimper his name.

He groans, deep and guttural. "You like that? You like when I fuck you like this?"

"Yes! Oh God, yes…"

"Then take it," he growls, hips pumping faster. "Take everything. It's yours. Only yours."

My climax hits like lightning, sudden and electric. My entire body tightens around him, a resounding cry leaving my mouth.

He curses and shouts my name, crashing into his own release, hips jerking as he spills inside me, still grinding through the aftershocks as if he can't bear to leave my body.

When he finally collapses on top of me, we're both gasping and sweating.

He brushes a kiss against my cheek, then my neck, then my lips.

"You okay?" he whispers.

I nod, dizzy from pleasure, blissfully sore. "More than okay."

He cups my face, thumb brushing my lips.

"Then stay with me. Please."

I reach up and take his face in both hands, pressing my mouth to his.

"Always."

In the middle of the night, he wakes me gently, then carries me to the shower.

The water hisses to life. Steam rises around us.

Noah pins me gently to the tiles, kissing me like he needs to memorize the shape of my mouth. Then he drops to his knees.

I barely have time to gasp before his mouth is on me. The sound I make, wild and shamelessly loud, doesn't even feel like mine. One of my hands claws at the fogged glass wall, the other tangles in his hair.

I've never felt anything like this. He devours me, half-asleep and trembling, my knees draped over his shoulders.

When I come, it's like I've been broken into pieces and rebuilt all at once. I sag against him as he rises and puts his arms around my waist, kissing my shoulders, my breasts.

He turns me carefully, bracing me against the wall. His hand finds its way between my legs, stroking and petting the wetness there that has everything to do with him.

He buries his face at the back of my neck, teeth nipping softly at the skin. "Tell me you want this."

"I want this," I breathe. "I want you."

When he pushes inside me from behind, I cry out.

Not in pain. Not even in fear. In wonder.

It doesn't hurt the way I thought it would.

It feels like finding a place where I am wanted without question, where I can feel without fear.

His other hand finds my breast, the other rubs me relentlessly as he moves. I fall into the rhythm of him, mouth open, eyes closed, every breath a prayer I don't know how to say.

And when he comes inside me, when his fingers and the length of him bring me to the peak, I scream his name as we pump against each other, falling with the cresting wave that only the two of us can ride.

I hear him say it as his arms circle my waist, as he kisses my wet hair tenderly.

"I love you, baby. I love you."

CHAPTER 6

The Surrender

I DECIDE I WANT TO OWN THIS.

Noah wraps me in a towel and carries me back to the bed. Although drenched and practically boneless, I toss the towel aside and climb on top of him.

"I want to see you," I say, "from here."

I sink down just above his hips and he curses, gripping my thighs tightly. My hands cradle his face, my breasts push against his chest, and I kiss him deeply.

"You're beautiful like this," I whisper, grinding my hips against his.

I feel him stirring back to life. My body responds with

the now-familiar heat pooling between my legs, ready for him once more.

"So are you," he mutters.

His hands find my breasts, rolling my nipples between his fingers. I gasp, rolling my hips in response, chasing the friction that I have come to know intimately that night.

My body burns, but in the best way.

"Say it, Noah," I tell him as I take him into my body, as I surrender to the dark, delicious depths of the man who watched me from the shadows and, somehow, loved me.

"I love you," he growls. "I fucking love you."

I thrust my hips against his, up and down, to the music of the rain, to the sound of his curses and his gasps.

And I say it.

"I love you too."

He grins, his hands digging into my hips. "About fucking time."

I squeal as he pumps into me, and I meet him in the middle of our rhythm.

We move together, faster and harder, and I don't care if the whole damn world hears me screaming his name.

I want this carved into my memory. I want all of him carved into me.

Into the glass and the light and the shadows of me.

And as we fall together once more, it's the first time I have ever felt whole.

When I wake just before dawn, it isn't in my narrow boardinghouse room.

It's in long shadows and soft sheets, in a room too big, too sleek, windows opening out to the dark city skyline blurred with rain.

Memory comes in delicious, sinful snippets that make me sink back onto the bed.

I'm at Noah's place.

The other side of the bed is empty, but on the nightstand sits a steaming cup of coffee and a note in bold handwriting.

Stay. You're safe here.

Always.

Love, N.

I press the note to my chest.

For the first time in my life, the dark doesn't feel like it's swallowing me whole.

Because Noah stood in it with me.

And he never let go.

THE FIRE
BETWEEN US

CHAPTER 1

The Garden

T HE SOUND OF HIS VOICE RIPPLES THROUGH THE QUIET
of the garden.

"Viv? Something wrong?"

A shiver runs through me as a gust of wind unsettles
the warm summer evening, rustling the bougainvillea and
making the air feel suddenly cooler. I close my eyes, lean
back in the rocking chair, and let the darkness after sunset
press against me like a blanket.

The crickets are singing again, steady and endless, and
for a moment I pretend that's all there is—the song, the
night, the slow creak of wood beneath me.

The garden has always been my sanctuary. My mother's

roses, the scent of soil and old earth, the way shadows bend in the corners but never quite threaten. I've lost hours here, lulled by the familiar.

But tonight the calm feels fragile. Too easily broken.

"Viv?"

His hand lands gently on my arm, warm against my skin.

I open my eyes, push a stray strand of hair from my face, and look at him at last.

Lloyd.

He's been standing here for minutes, maybe more, watching me. Always watching. I wonder if he has guessed what I've been thinking.

How heavy the world feels. Or how brittle I am beneath the surface.

"Hi." My voice comes out softer than I want it to. "I thought you'd be packing for tomorrow's flight."

I stretch slowly, forcing myself into movement, forcing a smile. "It leaves early. And don't think you're skipping my Bon Voyage breakfast. You promised."

He smiles back, his brown eyes glinting like they carry some secret light of their own. Lloyd is handsome in a way that makes people look twice. Dark hair falling around his temples, profile carved in a classic kind of way, a face that would have been at home in an old black-and-white Sampaguita Pictures movie.

And yet, he doesn't belong here. Not in my quiet garden, not in this small town he'd long since outgrown.

"Your breakfast offer is something no sane man would refuse," he teases.

I snort and look away before he can read too much in my expression. "Flatterer."

But he doesn't let it go. He never does.

"What's wrong, Viv?" His voice is gentler now, but more insistent too. "Is something wrong?"

He's more sensitive than I give him credit for. He always has been.

"I haven't eaten much today," I admit, though it's only part of the truth. "Migraine. Takes the appetite away."

He studies me, then slips an arm around my shoulders. I let him, even though the weight of his arm feels both safe and suffocating. "You look pale. Come over to the house. My cousins brought a feast—*lechon, talaba,* the works. I came to see if you'd join us."

I shake my head. "Do you mind if I stay here a while?"

"No. Not at all."

So I rest my head against his shoulder anyway, my body betraying me. For a moment the pain in my skull eases, the scent of his cologne familiar and comforting. He hasn't changed it since college.

Then he clears his throat. "So, Viv."

Something in his tone makes me lift my head. He won't look me in the eyes.

"I hope things are okay with you," he says, too quickly. "You've got to take care of yourself. Tita Roma told me you stay up until dawn, drink coffee like water."

"I work better at night. You know that." My arms fold around me before I even think, shielding myself.

He sighs, then reaches for my hand. I pull it away.

"We're all concerned," he tries again. "Slow down. Don't be too hard on yourself."

"I like my work." My voice takes on an edge. The air between us turns brittle.

"Easy, Viv." He raises his hands like he's surrendering. "I don't want you angry at me for caring about you."

The words slam into me harder than they should.

Caring about you.

I don't let myself believe them. Not when belief could unravel me.

Lloyd has always cared. He's been there with the chocolates on my birthday, the flowers, the ridiculous cartoon cards that made me laugh when no one else could. His sudden return to my life this week has left me off balance, a strange mix of comfort and disquiet. He's been beside me every day, prying open the quiet corners I've built around myself.

"Please," he says. "Don't be mad."

I sigh. I can't fight him, not when he won't fight back. "I'm sorry. Migraines make me cranky."

"Don't apologize." He draws me close again, firmer this time, and presses a kiss against the side of my head.

It's a brotherly gesture. It always has been. We grew up like this. Same street, same schools, our mothers tied by grief and friendship as young widows. He's always been the boy next door, the one who never made me feel small even as he outpaced me in everything else.

I should resent him, but I don't.

Earlier this week, I let him read my draft pitches. He praised them with such sincerity it had left me stunned. Two days later, I was speaking with his editor on the phone, a woman with a kind, smooth voice who told me she was impressed with my samples.

Lloyd had done that. Without asking. Without warning.

Just like that, he had shifted the axis of my world.

But change has always scared me.

Because if he could step in and alter my life so easily, he could just as easily step out again.

And I would be left alone once more, in distance and silence.

CHAPTER 2

The Park

S HE'S ICE.

Not the Vivian I grew up with, the one who laughed too loud and argued with me over nothing just to win. Not the girl who scribbled poems in the margins of our journalism notes. Tonight she's quiet, withdrawn, her words clipped like she's holding them hostage.

And it cuts me.

Because being with her is the only part of this week that has felt real. The reason I traded two big stories, the reason I let my producer's messages go to voicemail, the reason I've ignored the little notes that keep slipping into my inbox.

We know where you live.

Stop writing.

Even the death threats feel distant here, in her garden, in her presence. But Viv, shutting herself off like this…that I can't handle.

I don't want to leave her in this state. Hell, I don't want to leave her at all.

"Why don't we go somewhere," I say, aiming for lightness, like old times. "I don't think I can stomach another bite of *lechon* if I want to run the marathon again."

Her shoulders tense. She pulls away, just enough for me to feel the loss.

Did I say something wrong? Do something? I replay the whole week in my head, every smile she gave me, every silence I filled, and I come up empty.

She hesitates. "Okay. But we need to be back before midnight. You know how our moms are."

Relief sparks in my chest. "The park, then?"

"Okay. Give me a minute. I'll meet you outside."

She slips into the house, leaving me with the echo of her absence.

I head next door, where the cousins are still raising hell. Someone's butchering 'Closer You and I' by Gino Padilla on the videoke, and the table's a mess of pork bones and empty oyster shells.

I grab my mother's car keys. "I'm driving out."

"You mean Lloyd's got a hot night with his girlfriend!" one of my cousins sings into the mic.

Catcalls erupt, whistles following me out the door. My face burns. If Vivian heard that, she'd kill me on the spot.

I make a mental note to ban them all from the house forever.

When I pull up to the gate, there she is. She's changed into jeans and a yellow blouse, hair loose and neatly combed, bag slung over her shoulder. The sight of her steals my breath for a second.

I back the car out quickly before the cousins notice her. She'd hate their attention, and she'd take it out on me.

We're on the coastal road in minutes. The night stretches wide and endless, the sea hidden but near. I glance at her. She's stiff, staring out the window, like she'd rather be anywhere but here.

"Remember when we used to take this car to the *arroz caldo* place?" I ask, trying to catch her smile.

Her lips twitch. "All night café. Too bad it closed down. Nobody makes chicken soup like that anymore."

"I remember," I say. "We'd pool our coins and split a serving."

Finally, she looks at me, her mouth softening into the smallest smile. "And split the egg. Yellow for me, white for you."

I laugh. "Still can't eat the yolk because of you."

The silence that follows isn't heavy. It's companionable, the way it used to be when we were younger, scribbling articles and sharing ice cream straight from the tub. I switch on the radio, soft music filling the car as the lights of the park appear ahead.

We pull into the lot. Couples linger under the lamps, families are scattered around the playground, but it's quiet enough. I step out, circle the car, open her door. My instinct is to offer my hand, but I stop myself. She flinched earlier, and the last thing I want is to drive her further into herself.

So I just walk ahead, to the wide stone platform by the sea. My chest eases when I hear her footsteps falling into place beside mine.

"I wish the rest of the gang were here," I say, pointing at the swings in the middle of the grassy playground. "Louie, Claire, Faye, Dale—they'd be fighting over those seats already."

Her shoulders loosen, the stiffness ebbing. "They have kids who fight over swings now. I saw Louie and his wife in church last month. Three kids. Can you believe it?"

"Maybe more than a few years have passed," I offer.

"Has it really been that long?" Her voice dips wistfully. "It feels like time moves without me. Like everyone's out there living their lives, and I'm stuck."

Her words stab deep. I stop walking. She does too.

What can I say? What can I do?

Then her hand finds mine, cool and trembling.

"I'm sorry," she whispers. "For ruining your last night here. I must sound so depressing."

"No." I squeeze her hand, fragile in mine. "You sound real."

"My problems aren't your problems."

I turn, really looking at her. The moon paints her in silver—dark hair framing her face, eyes more expressive and haunting than she realizes, beauty that aches to look at.

My Viv. Always my Viv.

And there's only one truth left in me.

"I could make them mine."

CHAPTER 3

The Sea

M Y HEART IS A DRUM IN MY CHEST, SO LOUD I'M SURE he can hear it.

I've been wading through dangerous waters all week. Now it feels like I've stumbled into the deep end, where my feet can't touch the ground.

Someone like Lloyd Mosquera isn't supposed to be here, with me.

He's supposed to be out there, on some high-flying assignment for his column and syndicated show 'Man on Fire,' his byline in bold, his words sparking outrage and

He's supposed to be untouchable. Larger than life. A man made of fire and ink and distance.

Not this real.

Not standing in front of me, with his eyes burning holes through me.

Not close enough to feel like he could rewrite everything I thought I knew about myself.

"You don't know what you're saying, Lloyd," I say, tearing my hand away and wrapping my arms around myself. It's my armor now, my default defense whenever he makes me feel too much.

It was a mistake coming here. I should have stayed in my garden, safe and small.

But Lloyd never lets go. Not in his writing, not in life.

He rounds on me, his voice raw but still controlled. "The least you could do is give me a little credit, Viv. I do know what I'm talking about sometimes."

"You think you know anything about me?" My voice cracks with the frustration boiling under my ribs. "That somehow, after a week, you could just…fix everything?"

His jaw tightens. He doesn't move, but I feel the force of him like a firestorm barely contained. "Is that what you think I want to do? Change your life? Play the hero?" His voice lowers, hotter and rougher this time. "I couldn't change anyone's life, Viv. Least of all yours."

"Then what do you want?" The tears sting, threatening to spill. I hate them. I hate him for pulling them out of me. "What do you want from me?"

His eyes soften, but his body hums with restraint, like he's one wrong word away from breaking. "I want to be in your life. Not to fix it, not to carry it, but just to be there. When you're stuck. When you can't move."

"Why?" My voice cracks like glass.

"You know why."

The words are a whisper, nearly swallowed by the crash of waves against stone. But I hear them. I feel them.

His gaze says the rest.

And something inside me breaks.

My arms fall to my sides. My knees threaten to give way. Breathing is suddenly impossible, because my chest isn't hollow anymore.

It's full. Too full.

Wonder. Disbelief. Heat. Love.

One spark, and I'm burning.

I don't know who moves first.

Him. Me. Both of us.

All I know is that his mouth is on mine, and I'm lost.

Lloyd kisses like he writes. Unyielding, relentless, pouring everything into it until you're drowning in his truth.

His hand buries itself in my hair, tugging me closer, tilting my head so he can claim me deeper. I gasp, and he swallows it whole, his tongue stroking against mine, setting me on fire.

My hands fist in his shirt, pulling him closer, closer still, until my body is pressed against the solid heat of his. He's all muscle, all strength, the scent of salt and him wrapping around me.

I melt, and he devours.

His mouth trails lower, nipping at the corner of my jaw, down the line of my throat. My head falls back, a shudder ripping through me as his lips burn against my skin.

"I hope you know what you're getting yourself into," I breathe.

His breath is hot against my jugular. "I know exactly where I'm meant to be."

And when he pulls back just enough to look at me, his eyes are molten even in the shadows of the platform.

For years I thought I'd lost him to the bigger world, to the bright lights and dangerous shadows he walked through so easily. I thought he'd left me behind.

But here he is.

And here I am.

My body is fire. My mind is static. Everything inside me says too much.

His hands are in my hair, down my back, gripping my waist with a kind of desperation that makes me feel weak and shaky. He catches me, hauling me against him, and I feel the hard, undeniable press of him through his jeans.

Heat floods me. My body aches for him in a way I can't hide.

"Lloyd," I whisper, half a warning, half a plea.

I know we're hidden from the rest of the world by the

seawall, but someone could easily walk down from the park and see us.

"Viv." His voice is ragged, breathless. "Tell me to stop and I will."

But I don't. I can't.

Not even with the risk of getting caught.

Instead, I grab his shirt and tug it up, my fingers skimming hot skin as I push it over his head. The sight of him steals my breath.

Moonlight spills on his broad chest, showing muscles tight from years of carrying the weight of his world. A faint scar slices across his ribs like proof of all the danger he never talks about.

"God," I murmur, tracing it before I can stop myself.

He catches my wrist, eyes blazing. "Not now." And then he's kissing me again, harder, his hands sliding under my blouse, palms burning against my bare skin.

I gasp when his thumbs brush the underside of my breasts, when his mouth leaves mine to trail fire down my throat. "Lloyd…"

"I've always wanted you, Viv," he groans against my skin. "Say you want me too."

"I want you." The words break out of me. "I want you, Lloyd."

That's all it takes.

He pushes me gently back against the cold stone wall of the platform, his mouth finding mine again, his hands tugging at my jeans, fumbling at the button until I help him. The air stings against my skin as he slides them down, his touch following.

My hands dive into his hair, pulling him closer as he presses his hips to mine. The friction makes me cry out, the sound lost in his kiss. He's hard and hot, grinding against me in a way that makes my whole body catch fire.

"Here?" I manage, breathless, half in disbelief.

"Here." His voice is breathless. "I can't wait, Viv. I've waited too long."

His hand slips under my panties, and I arch into him, a cry tearing from my throat as his fingers find me, stroke me, tease me. He knows exactly what he's doing, exactly how to unravel me. I cling to him, gasping, shuddering, my body already spiralling out of control.

And when I'm shaking apart in his arms, he whispers against my lips, "I've got you. Always."

I don't remember how his jeans come off, only the sound of the zipper, the rush of cool air, then the heat of him pressing against me. He looks into my eyes, waiting, trembling as hard as I am.

"Yes," I murmur. "Please."

And then he's inside me, filling me, stretching me until I can't breathe. I clutch his shoulders, nails biting into his skin, and he groans like he's breaking.

He thrusts into me, slow at first, then harder, deeper, each movement sending shockwaves through me. My back arches against the stone, my legs wrap tightly around his hips, pulling him closer and deeper.

"Viv," he gasps, burying his face in my neck. "God, Viv…"

"Don't stop," I beg, meeting him, moving with him, the rhythm building between us until it feels like the whole world has narrowed to his body, his breath, his lips whispering my name.

When release tears through me, it's like the sea itself has risen up to swallow me whole. I cry out his name, trembling, clinging to him as he follows me over the edge, his body shaking, his groan muffled against my skin.

We collapse together, tangled and breathless.

"I hope you know what this means," he says, reaching to trace the curve of my cheek.

"I do," I answer, my body still trembling, my heart still racing. "And I don't care."

Because even if his world is dangerous, even if his shadows follow me now, he knows I've chosen him.

And he's chosen me.

CHAPTER 4

The Shadows

S HE'S STILL TREMBLING WHEN I HOLD HER.

Her breath shudders against my chest, her body soft and pliant in my arms. I swear I could stay like this forever.

The crash of the sea behind us is steady, but all I hear is her heartbeat against mine.

My Viv.

I've wanted her for so long I almost can't believe she's real in my arms, her skin warm, her lips swollen, her scent and sweat all over me.

"I meant it," I say into her hair, my throat tight. "Every word."

Her fingers graze my jaw, and she looks at me like I'm both a miracle and a mistake. "I know."

The undoing in her eyes is enough to break me.

I should stop. I should protect her from this. I should protect her from me.

But I can't. I won't.

Because I know she's always been mine.

She kisses me again, slowly.

"Again," she says, so soft the sound is almost carried away by the wind.

I freeze. "Say what?"

She giggles, then nibbles at my lower lip and whispers, "Don't you dare hold back now, Mosquera."

"Fuck," I growl as she reaches for my cock, already hard again at her touch.

I lay her down on the cold stone. This time I taste every inch of her, mapping her skin with my mouth. Her blouse rides up, baring her to the night air, and I drag my lips down her chest, her ribs, listening to the way she gasps and arches for me.

"Lloyd…" The sound of my name from her lips nearly kills me.

"I wanna taste you, Viv," I rasp, mouth teasing against her skin, until it finally reaches the wetness between her thighs.

I nip and suck, tongue drawing circles, breath tickling the soft, thin hair that carries her scent of roses and dew.

She lets out a strangled cry, hips buckling. "*Lloyd. Please.*"

I growl against her, my body burning.

Mine.

She's mine now.

When I slide back into her, it's deeper and slower, a claiming as much as a surrender. Her legs tighten around me, and I bury my face against her neck as I move inside her, slow at first, then harder and faster, until we're both coming apart together.

We collapse again, tangled and slick with sweat, her chest rising against mine. I press kisses into her hair, her temple, her mouth, drinking her in to convince myself that everything I ever wanted is now in my arms.

I don't know how long we stay like that. Time feels suspended, caught between her heartbeat and mine.

Eventually, I force myself to say, "We should go."

My chest aches with the words. Leaving feels like cutting a vein open.

She nods reluctantly, and I help her up, smoothing her hair, steadying her when her knees wobble. We laugh quietly at ourselves as we help each other dress, then walk back to the car. My fingers stay twined with hers, unwilling to let go.

But just as I open her door, my phone buzzes. The screen lights up.

Unknown number.

My stomach clenches. I see the message and my jaw locks tight. I shove the phone back into my pocket before she can read the words.

We saw you tonight. Enjoy. We'll be waiting.

"Work?" she asks, her voice soft, almost drowsy.

"Something like that," I mutter, squeezing her hand before I can stop myself. Then I force a smile I don't feel. "Nothing for you to worry about."

But I do worry. Because the shadows I've been keeping at bay just saw the one thing they can use against me.

I slide behind the wheel. Her hand rests on my thigh, and when I lace my fingers over hers, I swear I'll burn the world before I let anyone touch her.

As we pull away from the park, I know that this is only the beginning.

The beginning of us.

The beginning of whatever storms come with my name.

I can already feel the weight of them pressing closer. Unknown numbers, threats on smuggled notes, whispers from strangers on the street.

They're the kind of enemies who don't stop until they've gutted you.

But tonight I have her hand in mine, her warmth still on my skin, her trust burning in my heart.

I know I'll never let her go. Not this time.

If the world wants a war, it will get one.

Because wherever I go next, whatever shadows rise to meet me, she is coming with me.

THE
ROOMMATE
AGREEMENT

CHAPTER 1

Not A Girl

S HE ARRIVES AT DAWN.

When I first meet Joni, she's standing in the doorway of the apartment with her arms crossed, staring at me like she's seen a ghost.

"You're…Leslie Lim?"

I nod, bleary-eyed from interrupted sleep, still exhausted from the previous day of grad school classes, teaching Karate, and working at the restaurant.

"Yeah. Last I checked."

Her face twists. She takes a step back, almost tripping over the two battered suitcases behind her.

"You're—" Her face whitens as she breathlessly regains her balance. "Oh my God. You're a guy."

"And you thought I wasn't?"

"I thought you're a girl. Leslie…" She blows out a sharp breath, shoulders tight. "You know what, never mind."

She's smaller than I expected, pale in the harsh hallway light, with the kind of fragile frame that makes you think she could break under a hard wind. But her hair is a riot of dark curls, wild and stubborn, falling almost to her waist.

And those eyes…wide and unblinking, caught somewhere between fear and fight. They're the kind of eyes you don't forget, even if you try.

I tell myself I'm not looking. I tell myself I'm just being polite, that she's only a roommate, nothing more. But the truth is, something knocks loose in my chest, and I shove it down before it can take shape.

Because I don't do love at first sight. I don't do fragile girls who look like they've lived through more than they should.

And I definitely don't do the way my hands itch to reach out, to steady her.

So instead, I nod, forcing my voice to be calm and neutral.

"Let me guess," I say. "You're Joni Guevarra."

She nods. "This was supposed to be a practical arrangement. When Student Services said someone had a vacancy in their subsidized accommodation, I didn't think twice."

"It can still be practical," I say, trying to keep my voice calm. "I'll stay out of your way."

She mutters something under her breath, then exhales deeply. "Good. I'd like that."

I step aside to let her in.

As soon as she's inside the apartment, I move to the hallway to retrieve her suitcases.

"You don't have to," she says, staring at me again.

"It's okay. I got it."

Without another word—and without looking at her too hard—I bring her suitcases inside and show her to her room.

We make a roommate agreement that night, scribbled in her small, neat handwriting on the back of an old course syllabus:

1. *No visitors after midnight.*
2. *No entering each other's rooms.*
3. *No unnecessary talking.*
4. *No crossing personal lines.*

It's all rules, no warmth. She tapes it to the refrigerator door like some kind of gospel.

I don't argue.

I've lived by a stricter code my entire life.

CHAPTER 2

Not A Dream

Bᴜᴛ Jᴏɴɪ ɪsɴ'ᴛ ᴇᴀsʏ ᴛᴏ ɪɢɴᴏʀᴇ.

She's always up early for work at the university library and the graduate school office. She studies late into the night, books spread across the kitchen table like a fortress. She wears oversized hoodies that swallow her frame, and she chews the ends of her pens until the plastic bends.

And sometimes, I hear her.

Not her studying. Not her muttering over notes.

Her nightmares.

The first time, it's past two in the morning. I'm on the sofa, freshly showered after a long night at the restaurant for my boss' private engagement party, surfing through channels in an attempt to feel sleepy. But I can't fall asleep, a little too happy and excited at the money in the envelope I got as a bonus.

I'm about to message my mother, to tell her I'll be sending her dialysis money earlier that month, when I hear muffled cries bleed through the wall.

It's followed by a choked plea.

"Stop…please stop."

I find myself standing outside her door, fist hovering over wood, debating on what I should do.

Rule Number Two says no entering. But rules don't mean much when someone sounds like they're drowning.

I knock softly. "Joni? You okay?"

The sound cuts off.

There's silence, followed a shaky breath.

"I'm fine."

She's not. But I back away.

Over the weeks, I learn pieces.

Not from her telling me, but from what slips through the cracks.

The way she flinches when a door slams too hard in the hallway.

The way her hands tremble when she hears a man raise his voice, even if it's just people passing outside on the street or an actor on TV.

The way she triple checks the locks on the apartment door before going to bed.

And one night, when the nightmare is worse than usual, I hear her say, *"Don't lock us in, Papa. Please don't."*

My chest burns. I know then.

She didn't just run to grad school for ambition.

She ran to survive.

Despite the rules, we keep colliding.

She makes coffee. I make eggs. She offers me a mug. I offer to make her sunny side-up. We end up eating together in silence.

She hogs the washing machine. I fold her clothes without asking, and she glares but doesn't stop me.

She steals my spare pens. I hide her favorite mug, just to see her scowl.

It's far from a romance. It's not even friendship. It's something raw and jagged in between.

And every time our hands brush—passing a plate, reaching for the fridge handle—something inside me stirs.

Something I'm not supposed to want.

It breaks one night after I come back from the restaurant, still sporting bruised knuckles from sparring earlier that day in preparation for a tournament I'm training the bigger kids in.

She's on the couch, legs curled under her, staring at the blank TV screen.

"You okay?" I ask.

She doesn't answer. Instead, she looks at my hands. "Does it hurt?"

I shrug. "Not really. I'm used to it. Been into Karate since I was four. Teaching since I was eighteen."

She nods. "You had dinner yet? I have some extra *pancit* put aside."

The question makes me freeze midway to my room.

I nod, swallowing hard. "Yeah. Our boss lets us have whatever we want to eat before going home. Saves a lot of money that way, to be honest."

She averts her eyes. "You heard me the other night, didn't you?"

I stare at her. "Heard you?"

Then, in a voice almost too soft for me to hear, she adds, "I used to hear my mother scream when my father hit her. My brother and I were locked in my room. He was younger, so I'd cover his ears. But I heard everything. Every hit."

The air thickens.

I sit down across from her. Not too close, but close enough.

"You're safe now, Joni," I say. "No one's going to hurt you. Not while you're with me."

Her laugh is sharp and bitter. "Safe doesn't stick, Les. It just…slips away."

I want to tell her I'll hold it steady. That I'll fight off every ghost her father ever planted. But I don't.

Instead, I reach over and take her hand. She tenses, but she doesn't pull away.

Her skin is cold. Mine is warm.

Slowly, she lets her fingers curl into mine.

She lifts her eyes, meeting my own. "Has anyone ever told you?"

"Told me what?"

For the first time, I see a smile bloom across her face.

"You look a lot like J-Hope."

CHAPTER 3

Not A Rule

THE AGREEMENT BEGINS TO UNRAVEL AFTER THAT. We talk more. We eat together. We sit in silence that isn't empty anymore.

She tells me that her father died from lung cancer last year, and her mother is still teaching at the public elementary school in Kalibo. Her brother is in college at a neighboring district, studying to become a merchant marine. He actually helped her find a job at the university, since the mother of his best friend works at the same place.

I tell her about my father who left us for another woman when I was six, and my mother who used to run a small *manokan* in Bago City before she got too sick to cook. I tell her how Karate got me out of trouble when I was younger, and how I got my first job because of it.

I find out we both want to teach. Maybe abroad.

And one night, after another nightmare, she comes out of her room and knocks on my door at three in the morning. Her eyes are wet, her curls a wild mess.

She doesn't say anything. She just stands there, shaking.

I open my arms.

She steps into them.

The hug is awkward at first, stiff, all edges and hesitation. Then she buries her face against my chest, and I feel her breathe against me, the sound ragged and uneven.

My shirt dampens with her tears. My hand finds the back of her head.

"No one's going to hurt you, Joni," I tell her. "You're safe with me."

She clings tighter.

Then, on my bed, she cries herself to sleep.

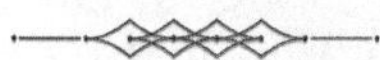

From then on, the lines blur.

She tells me she will become too fat because of how well I cook, but eats everything I make for her. I tease her about her caffeine addiction, but she still brings me coffee every single time she makes some for herself.

She sits in the corner of the dojo sometimes while I teach, watching me like she doesn't know if she's impressed or terrified.

She times her trips to Megaworld with my shifts at the restaurant so she's waiting for me when I get off work. One warm summer evening, my boss' fiancée sees her standing outside and admires her curly hair, then invites Joni in for some ice cream, thinking she's my girlfriend. No one admits or denies anything.

We study together, and find out we're both fans of the Korean action series *The Uncanny Counter*. I tell her the noodle chef lady reminds me of my mother.

And when she dreams bad, she comes to me. Always to me.

The night it all tips over, she's sitting on my bed, knees drawn up, wearing one of my shirts because hers is in the laundry pile. The hem brushes her thighs, and she's chewing her lip like she's daring herself to speak.

"I hate rules," she mutters.

"Then break them." My voice is low, rougher than I mean it to be.

Her head snaps up, eyes wide. Something flickers there—fear, want, maybe defiance—and before I can second-guess it, she leans in and kisses me.

It's clumsy at first, rushed, all teeth and nerves. But the second her lips soften, I ease back, gentling it. My hand cradles the side of her face, fingers brushing her cheek.

She shivers under my touch. "Les…"

"Shhh." I put my arms around her, steadying us both. "We don't have to rush. You call the pace. You tell me what you want."

Her breath hitches, then she kisses me again, firmer and

hungrier this time. The sound that escapes her throat is half a whimper, half a demand.

I pull her closer. She fits against me like she's been meant to all along.

"Tell me what to do, Joni," I murmur against her mouth. "It's all about you."

She shakes her head, fingers coaxing the hem of my own shirt upward. "Don't let me go."

And I don't.

I kiss her slowly, deeply, letting her set the rhythm. My hand strokes up her thigh, delving past the fabric of her shorts, careful and tentative at first. When she tilts her hips closer, I take it as permission.

Her breath comes faster, her hands clutching at my clothes, pulling them off with a raw, almost desperate need, until I'm naked.

She helps me undress her, pulling off the borrowed shirt to reveal her bare, perfectly round breasts. Her shorts and panties follow.

I take in the sight of her, feeling dizzy and a little overwhelmed, and draw her close.

"You're safe," I whisper, lips tracing her jaw, her throat. "With me, you're always safe."

Her nails dig into my back as she arches against me, pressing her hips to mine. "Then make me feel it. Tonight. Always."

Something in me breaks loose at those words.

Tenderness changes into heat, the kind that coils low in

my stomach. I ease her back onto the mattress, our mouths never parting. She pulls me with her, tugging until my weight settles above her.

The kiss grows fiercer, more desperate, and when she moans into my mouth, I nearly lose it. My hands roam, hers too, until I am rock-hard, until she is warm and soaking wet against me.

Every wall she's built between us crumbles piece by piece, replaced by the way she molds her body against mine, the way she gasps my name, the way she tells me to make her feel everything.

And when we finally cross that last line together, when she lets me take her and I obey her cries for more, it isn't just about breaking rules anymore.

It's about us rewriting everything.

The roommate agreement is still taped to the refrigerator door the next morning.

The first four rules are crossed out now.

But at the bottom, in her handwriting, a new line has appeared.

5. *Don't ever let me go.*

And every time I see it, I know I never will.

SUNSETS IN SEPTEMBER

CHAPTER 1

Another Year

Every September, I return.

The pier is the same as it was the day he first brought me here.

The wooden planks are still weathered by salt, while sea spray still mists the air. I can still hear fishermen's laughter echoing down the rails.

My fiancé used to say this place feels like forever.

But forever never came.

He died in a highway accident three years ago.

But I still come on his birthday and stay for a few days.

Every day I'm here, I sit at the edge of the pier with a paper cup of coffee, watch the sun burn the sea gold, and pretend he's beside me.

Only this year, I'm not alone.

There's a man standing at the rail, hands in his pockets, shoulders broad under a navy button-down. His presence is quiet but steady. He glances at me once—dark eyes, sharp looking but tired—and nods.

I nod back.

That's all. But it's enough to unsettle the rhythm of my ritual.

The next evening, he's there again.

"Hi," he says, voice deep and even.

"Hi."

We stand side by side, not quite close but not far. He smells faintly of something cool and smoky.

On the third evening, he says, "You come here often?"

"Every September," I admit. "This is my third."

His lips twitch, like he understands more than I said. "My first time this year."

There's silence. The sea roars before us. I want to ask him why, but something in his face, one deeply etched with lines of time and loss, stops me.

We don't trade stories.

Just quiet nods, shared sunsets, and the small comfort of knowing someone else carries ghosts too.

CHAPTER 2

Another Ending

O N MY LAST NIGHT, THE PIER IS BUSIER THAN USUAL. The planks are packed with vendors selling grilled corn, peanuts, and balloons. Couples and families walk around leisurely, admiring the view at high tide, while kids run about barefoot. The promise of rain hangs heavy in the air.

I linger longer than usual, waiting for the sky to turn the color he loved, blazing orange fading into deep purple. It's like saying goodbye, in a way.

Another end to another year.

When I finally turn toward the narrow road leading back

to town where my pension house is, I don't notice the man shadowing me until his hand snatches at my bag.

I stumble, shouting, clutching the strap as panic explodes in my chest.

Then suddenly, he's there.

The man from the pier.

Moving faster than I can blink, he twists the snatcher's wrist, wrenches my bag free, and sends the thief stumbling into the sand. The snatcher curses and bolts into the dark.

I'm left gasping, clutching my bag, staring at him.

"Are you okay?" he asks, voice firm and steady.

"I…yes," I breathe out. "Yes. I think so."

He exhales, the coiled tension seemingly leaving his body. He pulls a badge from his back pocket and flashes it briefly. "I'm a cop. Senior Inspector Brian Medina."

It all clicks into place—the way he carries himself, the way he moved so quickly and effortlessly.

"I'm…Meera. Attorney Meera Fabregas."

He extends a hand, a little formally. "It's nice to meet you."

I take it, my palm disappearing underneath his. His grip is firm, but somehow gentle. "Nice to meet you too. Thanks for your help."

He shakes his head. "I'm sorry I wasn't able to reach him earlier. I could have caught him before he did that to you."

I stare at him. "Have you been…watching me?"

His jaw flexes. He hesitates for a moment before he answers.

"Yes. I wanted to make sure you were safe. From the first day."

He offers to walk me to the pension house. We make our way together back toward town, taking the boardwalk route that skirts the beach.

My knees are still weak from the encounter, but his presence steadies me.

"Why September?" I ask finally, voice trembling.

His silence is long. Then, he says softly, "It's my wife's birthday yesterday. She passed away almost two years ago. Cancer." His tone is matter-of-fact, but his eyes are raw. "I came here because this place was her favorite view. We had our honeymoon in a resort nearby. She used to say sunsets made her believe in happy endings. Riding off into the sunset, all that. She owned a flower shop."

I swallow hard. "My fiancé loved sunsets too. He…he died in a crash. I work in the city, but I come back for his birthday. This is his hometown. And the pier was where he proposed to me."

We stop walking. For the first time, we truly face each other. Two people bound by grief, standing in the golden afterglow of a sun that refuses to linger.

"I'm sorry for your loss," he says.

"I'm sorry for your loss, too," I echo quietly. "Your wife sounds like a wonderful lady."

He gives me a small, sad smile. "You could say she was a romantic."

I smile. "She's right. We didn't get our happy endings, but sunsets do make you believe in them. They're always something to look forward to, in spite of everything."

He nods. "They're like second chances, I guess."

I look at the darkening horizon, then at him, tilting my head. "You can say that. I believe in second chances. Maybe that's why I became a lawyer."

Neither of us say anything for several long moments, then I take a deep breath and continue. A part of me wants him to know. To understand.

"Years ago, a very good friend of mine was killed in a robbery. His brother found the men who did it and finished them all off. I knew he did what he did out of love, so I did everything I could to make sure he got out of prison early. He and his wife have a son now. She's going to take the Bar exams next year. Hopefully she'll become a lawyer too."

Brian leans over and takes my chin in his hand. "I have never heard of anything more romantic than that, coming from a lawyer."

I laugh, blushing at this new, strange kind of connection. "Look at us. Old romantics."

I find myself caught by the way his eyes soften when they rest on me as he moves closer.

It's not pity, but recognition. A mirror of everything I've carried alone.

I don't know who moved first, but when his lips touch mine, it isn't fire at first.

It's a spark, cautious and waiting.

He's giving me time to pull away. To say no.

But I kiss him back. Harder.

And that's when the spark catches.

He groans low in his throat, one hand rising to cradle my cheek, the other moving around my waist to pull me closer. His thumb brushes my skin gently, even as his mouth moves with growing urgency against mine.

I clutch his shirt tightly, panting, and ask, "Do you want to come with me? For coffee?"

Just as breathlessly, he answers, "Yes."

CHAPTER 3

Another Beginning

MY LEGS DON'T STOP SHAKING, EVEN WHEN WE REACH my room at the pension house.

My fingers fumble the keys, but his hand covers mine, steady and firm, guiding the door open. He reaches up to flip on the light, a soft golden glow settling over the tiny space.

Inside, it feels too quiet. Too small. My pulse won't slow.

I set my bag down on the table, my breath still ragged.

I turn and look at him standing at the threshold—the buttons at his collar undone, the storm still raging in his eyes—and I realize exactly what I feel.

It's something I haven't felt in years. Something I never gave myself the permission to feel again.

It's want. It's need.

And it's the last thing from coffee.

Because it's him.

The door clicks shut behind him, and suddenly it's just us and the sound of the sea, muffled through the open window.

The words escape before I can stop them.

"I don't want to be alone tonight, Brian."

His silence is heavy, eyes locking onto mine. Then he steps closer, close enough that I feel his heat.

"Neither do I."

The kiss is molten, a clash of everything unsaid, a dam of the years breaking wide open.

His mouth claims mine with burning heat, his hands anchoring my waist. I gasp against him, and he deepens it, tongue sliding past my lips, tasting me.

I clutch at his shirt, feeling the solid muscle beneath, the tension coiled and breaking free. He lifts me easily, settling me on the edge of the bed without breaking the kiss.

"Meera," he murmurs against my throat. His hand slides down my arm, to my waist, pausing as if to ask permission. "Tell me if you want this. If not, I'll leave."

"Yes," I answer, arching into his touch. "I want this. I want you."

I shiver as he starts to bare my body, not just the skin

but the parts of myself I've hidden for years. He pauses, eyes dark as he takes in the sight of my breasts, still partially covered by my lace bra.

"You're beautiful, Meera," he says, as if it's the simplest truth.

My throat tightens. I don't remember the last time anyone looked at me this way.

He undresses me slowly, kissing each new stretch of skin. When his palm cups my bare breasts then moves to the heat between my legs, and when his mouth follows, I gasp out his name again and again, clutching his shoulders.

He doesn't stop there. His lips trail fire on my skin, then he slides lower, pushing my legs apart.

"You're so beautiful," he says again, voice gravelly with desire. "I want to taste all of you."

"Brian…" My eyes widen, and I almost scream when his mouth finds me.

But he is as steady as the tide.

His tongue and lips move relentlessly over that achingly wet part of me, flicking and swirling in maddening rhythm. His fingers follow, and I come undone, legs shooting into the air as he licks me clean, even as I shake and whimper under his touch.

His clothes come off then, one piece at a time. His body is warm and bronze, hard with muscle and discipline. In contrast, mine is soft, pale, trembling with need.

The contrast feels electric.

I trace the lines of his chest, his back, the ridges of

strength I've only imagined. He shivers under my touch. Boldly, I reach for him, too, with both hands, rubbing and stroking the rigid length between my palms.

When he finally enters me, it's slow and tender, a stretch that steals my breath. He holds still, forehead pressed to mine, waiting.

"Okay?" he whispers.

"Yes," I whisper back, wrapping my legs around his hips, taking him deeper into me.

He moves carefully, each thrust measured, as if he's determined not to break me. But soon his control melts into hunger, and the rhythm deepens. Our bodies find a pace that feels like waves—rolling, building, crashing.

I cling to him, nails in his back, gasping with every surge. He groans into my ear, muttering my name, growling and groaning as he comes apart in my arms.

It's not just sex.

It's choosing life again, together, in the dark of a seaside hotel.

When release finally takes me, it rips through me like a tidal wave.

He follows, holding me tightly, as if I'll drift away if he doesn't.

"Meera," he murmurs into my ear as we both ease down from the high of our shared pleasure. "Stay. Stay with me."

"Yes," I answer. "Yes."

Early morning light seeps slowly into the room, soft and tinged with gray.

I wake up curled against his chest, his arm heavy around me, protective even in sleep.

For one suspended breath, I fear he'll be gone when I blink. But when I stir, he does too, eyes opening, warm and unguarded.

"Good morning," he rasps.

Relief and something wilder flood me. I smile broadly. "Good morning."

"You stayed," he says, smiling back.

I prop myself up over his chest, nuzzling my nose against his. "Of course I stayed."

His thumb strokes my cheek in slow, lingering circles. Then he glances toward the pale blush of dawn outside the window.

"We've been chasing sunsets," he murmurs. "Chasing ghosts. Maybe it's time to try something else."

I frown slightly. "Like what?"

His lips curve with something almost shy. "What if we watched the sunrise together instead? A new day. A new start."

A lump rises in my throat, but it's not grief. Tears slip free anyway, soft and grateful.

"Yes," I answer. "I'd like that very much."

He kisses me tenderly then, his fingers gently brushing away my tears.

It feels like a promise.

It feels like a chance at something new.

And when we step out to the balcony hand in hand, the horizon blooms with light.

Not in farewell, but in welcome.

ABOUT THE AUTHOR

Shirley Siaton writes edgy and evocative novels and poems. Her worlds are in a deliciously dark cross-section of the romance, neo-noir, action, contemporary, and fantasy genres. Her background in various Asian martial arts inspires a lot of her work.

She has several books of fiction and poetry released since February 2023. Her first book is the free verse collection *Black Cat and other poems. Befallen* (March 2025) is her first full-length novel. She also pens juvenile literature as Shirley Parabia.

She is an award-winning writer, poet, and journalist in English, Filipino, and Hiligaynon. Her essays, short stories, and poems have been published internationally in print and digital media. Her multi-lingual plays have been staged in the Philippines.

Shirley is a black belt in Shotokan Karate and an international certified fitness coach. She has a Master's degree in Public Administration and works in education, wellness, and publishing. Originally from Iloilo City, she lives in the Middle East with her husband and two daughters.

ON THE WEB

Shirley's official website:
shirleysiaton.com

Complete reading guide:
shirley.pub

Subscribe to Shirley's VIP list for free exclusive updates:
newsletter.shirleysiaton.com